SPECIAL MESSAGE TO READERS

THE ULVERSCROFT FOUNDATION
(registered UK charity number 264873)
was established in 1972 to provide funds for
research, diagnosis and treatment of eye diseases.
Examples of major projects funded by
the Ulverscroft Foundation are:-

- The Children's Eye Unit at Moorfields Eye Hospital, London
- The Ulverscroft Children's Eye Unit at Great Ormond Street Hospital for Sick Children
- Funding research into eye diseases and treatment at the Department of Ophthalmology, University of Leicester
- The Ulverscroft Vision Research Group, Institute of Child Health
- Twin operating theatres at the Western Ophthalmic Hospital, London
- The Chair of Ophthalmology at the Royal Australian College of Ophthalmologists

You can help further the work of the Foundation
by making a donation or leaving a legacy.
Every contribution is gratefully received. If you
would like to help support the Foundation or
require further information, please contact:

THE ULVERSCROFT FOUNDATION
The Green, Bradgate Road, Anstey
Leicester LE7 7FU, England
Tel: (0116) 236 4325

website: www.foundation.ulverscroft.com

DUST AND BULLETS

Falsely accused of the murder of his partner, Ben Arrowsmith, Dan Fogarty escapes arrest and heads for cactus country to join his old Navajo friend, Ahiga. Dan suspects that the notorious outlaw the Ocotillo Kid is responsible for his partner's death, but when he and Ahiga set out to prove it, they run into more questions than answers. What is the relationship between the Ocotillo Kid and local magnate Wes Baxter? And why would the ruthless gangster take the trouble to frame Dan?

Books by Vance Tillman
in the Linford Western Library:

RIDERS ON THE WIND

VANCE TILLMAN

DUST AND BULLETS

Complete and Unabridged

LINFORD
Leicester

First published in Great Britain in 2013 by
Robert Hale Limited
London

First Linford Edition
published 2015
by arrangement with
Robert Hale Limited
London

A catalogue record for this book is available
from the British Library.

ISBN 978–1–4448–2287–8

1

Dan Fogarty was standing at the bar of the Hungry Loop saloon when he heard the batwings creak and the heavy thud of boots. He raised his glass but before he had time to take a drink he felt the muzzle of a gun in his back.

'Don't try anythin',' a voice snarled. 'Just untie your gunbelt and hand it to my deputy.' Fogarty didn't argue the point. 'OK, now start walkin'.'

'Where are we goin'?' Fogarty said.

'To the jailhouse.'

Fogarty looked into the faces of the marshal and his deputy. The marshal's features were lined and his hair was grey; the deputy looked like a tenderfoot. 'Are you goin' to tell me what this is all about?' he asked.

'I think you know what it's about,' the marshal replied.

'Not unless you got some kinda law

sayin' a man ain't allowed a drink,' Fogarty countered.

The marshal looked him in the eye. 'Don't play games,' he said. 'You know as well as I that you murdered your partner, Ben Arrowsmith, and took his share of the gold you found up in the hills.'

Fogarty felt as though he had been punched in the stomach. 'Ben,' he muttered. 'Murdered? I don't understand.'

'You don't fool me,' the marshal said. 'I've seen the body. And what's more, I got a witness.'

Fogarty was trying to come to terms with what the marshal was telling him. 'Where's the body?' he managed to say.

'Where you killed him; we buried him by the Senita River.'

The shock Fogarty felt lasted for only a moment. Before he made to step away from the bar he was already figuring his next move. He certainly had no intention of going to jail, especially now he knew what he was being accused of.

Once behind bars, he would have no chance of proving his innocence. With a shrug, he moved away from the bar and walked slowly through the room. He was aware of eyes watching him but he didn't look to either right or left. All his attention was concentrated on what he would do when he reached those batwing doors. He had taken good note of the layout of the town when he rode in and he knew there was an alley immediately to the left of the saloon. It led to some stores and a livery stable, behind which there were woods. He calculated times and distances, all the while moving at as slow a pace as he could. Outside, over the batwings, he could see that it was growing dark.

He was almost at the batwings when he suddenly sprang forward, hurling himself through them. They swung back, catching the marshal a glancing blow. As he dashed into the alleyway a gun exploded behind him and a bullet smacked into the corner stanchion of the saloon. He began to zigzag. A further shot rang out, but it was even darker in the alley than it was in the main street and he wasn't an easy target. In a few seconds he had reached the end of the alley. Without looking or slackening his pace, he made for the open door of the livery stable. He heard a shout and the whinny of a horse and glanced up to see a wagon looming over him. He stumbled and almost went under the front wheels, but regained his balance and carried on.

Another shot boomed and the horse reared. The wagon swerved, blocking the roadway. Fogarty was already through the wide-open doors of the livery stable. The ostler stood in his way but he brushed the startled man aside and ran on through the back entrance. Outside there was a corral with some horses. Without pausing he vaulted the rail. For a moment he considered leaping on the back of one of the horses but thought better of it. Instead, he sprang over the rail at the other side. It was only a short distance to the trees and he had reached their shelter before a fresh burst of gunfire told him the marshal must have disentangled himself from the obstruction caused by the wagon. It didn't concern him. The trees protected him and he was confident of being able to outmanoeuvre both the marshal and his deputy. He also had an odd feeling that the marshal was holding something back, that he could have shot him if he had really wanted to. Or maybe it was his deputy who had fired the shots. He carried on running and didn't stop till he was well clear of the town. Night had descended. He had escaped, but he knew he would have to go back for his horse.

The marshal was no fool. Once Fogarty had made it to the woods he knew there was no chance of catching him. His deputy was keen to carry on the chase, but the marshal shook his head.

'Leave it for now,' he said. 'He won't get far away without guns or a horse. If it proves necessary, we'll get up a posse in the morning.'

They turned away and walked back to the marshal's office. The air inside was stale with heat and the smell of tobacco. The deputy was still carrying Fogarty's gunbelt and he hung it over a nail on the wall.

'He can't cause too much trouble without his guns,' he said.

'You can go now, Somersby,' the marshal said.

'Isn't there somethin' we should be doin'?'

'All in good time. Like I say, there'll be plenty of opportunity to catch up with Fogarty tomorrow.'

Somersby was hesitant but finally moved towards the door. 'See you tomorrow, then,' he said.

'Sure thing. Be prepared to do some ridin'.'

When the door had closed the marshal sat down at his desk and opened a drawer. He had other things to worry about. He drew out a poster and looked at it closely. *Wanted: Dead or Alive.* The man's name was Ike Goffin, but he was better known as the Ocotillo Kid. It seemed he was on the loose again with a bunch of real hardcases gathered round him. How long would it be before he and his gang showed up in Hackberry? The marshal's deputy, Somersby, was a novice. If trouble brewed, real trouble, how would he shape up?

The marshal could ask the same question of himself. The town had been relatively peaceful for a long time. Maybe he had grown rusty. Maybe he wasn't the man he used to be. In the old days it had been him alone. Now he had someone else to worry about: his niece, Cora Siddons, was due later in the week on the stage from Dry Fork. Suddenly restless, he got to his feet and peered out of the grimy window. The blackness was relieved by pools of light spilling from the buildings. Leaving the Wanted poster on his desk, he turned down the lamp and stepped out into the night, locking the door behind him.

Fogarty wasn't too concerned about being recognized when he slipped back into Hackberry. There was still more than an hour before dawn and the streets were dark and deserted. Getting his horse was the easy part. He had left it, not at the main livery stable, but at a smaller one near the edge of town. Retrieving his weapons was more difficult. He considered breaking into the gun store, but he had a liking for his own familiar .44 Frontier model Colts. They would be at the marshal's office. As he made his way there, slipping like a ghost through the inky black shadows, he suddenly flinched as something moved in front of him. A dark shape sprang out from under his feet, but he realized it was only a cat.

He arrived outside the door of the marshal's office and gave it a tug. Of course, it was locked. He had no alternative but to break in. What did it matter anyway? He was already a wanted man on a charge of murder. Taking a stone from his pocket, he hurled it through the window. In a matter of seconds he had climbed through.

He took a quick glance around. A shaft of moonlight fell on the wall and he saw his gunbelt where the deputy had hung it. As he crossed the room he stumbled against the table where the marshal had left the poster. He stopped for a moment, rubbing his thigh. His eye fell on the poster and he held it up to the light. He could dimly make out the features of the man it depicted, together with the larger lettering. It didn't make a lot of sense to him but for some reason he folded it over and put it in the inside pocket of his jacket. Then he took down his gunbelt and strapped it round his waist. He made his way back to the window and peered outside. Nothing was stirring; no one had heard the sound of breaking glass.

He hoisted himself up, clambered over the window ledge and dropped down onto the boardwalk. Swiftly he made his way to the back of the livery stables where he knew he would find his horse, a bay roan, in an outside corral. His luck was in. He had thought he would have to break into the building itself to retrieve his saddle, but there was another one hanging draped across the top bar of the corral fence. He strapped it to the horse and then led the animal out into the narrow street beyond, where he stepped into the leather and rode off into the darkness.

He carried on riding through the rest of the night and didn't stop till around midday when he felt he had put sufficient distance between himself and Hackberry to feel safe. The marshal would realize what had happened as soon as he got back to his office. It was unlikely that he would waste time searching for him in the immediate environs of town, but it would take him a little time to get up a posse and Dan Fogarty was confident of being able to stay ahead of it. One man could travel a lot quicker than a bunch of riders. He stopped beside a brook and took out the makings. All the time he had been riding his thoughts had been churning over and he was grateful for the rest.

What was clear was the fact that his partner had been killed and he, Fogarty, was being held responsible. But who had informed the marshal? The marshal had mentioned a witness. Was that just bravado? Whoever had spread the malicious rumour must have made it sound very convincing. There had been a few prospectors working the river at the same time as he and his partner. Could it have been one of them?

When he had rolled his cigarette he reached into his pocket for a light and felt the Wanted poster. He drew it out and looked at it more closely. The face of the wanted man looked back at him, thin and wasted. He thought back to the morning of the day he had left the diggings. While he and his partner were having breakfast, a couple of riders had stopped by, asking the way to Hackberry. He hadn't taken too much notice

11

of the men; it was his partner who had spoken to them. One of the men, however, was unusually tall and lank. Spidery, like the ocotillo cactus. The poster said the Ocotillo Kid was wanted for murder and robbery. Was it just a coincidence that the Kid and his gang were apparently operating in the same area as he and his partner had been prospecting?

It was certainly worth following up, because he had no intention of letting the matter drop. Someone had killed his partner and he meant to find out just who it was. It wasn't a question of clearing his name. That thought didn't occur to him. It went a lot deeper than that. He owed it to his partner to bring his killer to justice. Like the poster said, he would bring him in, dead or alive. Right now he needed provisions. He needed a place to rest up where the marshal wouldn't find him.

As he turned the matter over he was struck by a sudden thought. His old friend Ahiga had moved down to the

Papago country and, unless he had drifted on again, he lived not too far away. It would take the rest of the day riding but he thought he could remember where the Navajo lived in the foothills of the Santa Catalina mountains. If Ahiga was no longer there, it wouldn't matter because he would still have put a lot more ground between himself and the marshal. He finished his cigarette, got to his feet and climbed back into the saddle.

*   *   *

The bay roan pulled up with its legs locked straight. Fogarty slid from the leather, moved to the edge of the plateau and looked down into the canyon. Far below was where his friend Ahiga had kept some sheep and tended a small orchard of peaches and plums with irrigation from a narrow wash. There was an almost inaccessible trail down and he let his horse pick its way. At the bottom the horse splashed

13

through the shallow waters of the wash until Fogarty saw the small log hogan standing about 200 yards back from the trail in the meagre shade of a twisted cottonwood. He got down from his horse and stooped to look inside.

There was no sign of the Navajo. Fogarty ducked back and, looking around, called his friend's name: 'Ahiga!' The sound echoed from the cliff but there was no other reply. Fogarty moved towards the little orchard. A trap had been set and although it was sprung, the trap was empty. Probably a raccoon or a skunk had been eating the fruit.

'Ahiga!' Fogarty called again. The cliffs threw the sound back at him. As he walked back to the hogan his horse snickered and the sound suddenly made him feel lonely. Almost unnoticed the night had come and the purple darkness was redolent with the scent of sage and dry grass. The place was spooky but he had been riding all day and he didn't relish travelling any further. The horse needed rest too. The hogan was as good a place as any to make camp. The fact that it was there at all suggested that Ahiga was still around.

Although he felt exhausted, he found it difficult to sleep. The hogan was small and oppressive. He felt shut in and oddly nervous. As he lay with his eyes closed, trying to shut out the thoughts that circled in his head, he suddenly tensed. He thought he had heard something outside. Instantly he was on his feet, his gun in his hand. He stepped to the side of the opening which passed for a door frame, listening intently. He could hear nothing further and had just about decided that he must have been mistaken when a dark figure slipped through the gap. As it did so, Fogarty stepped out into the open.

'Put your hands up,' he snapped. The man raised his arms. 'Turn round and make it slow.' The man turned and even in the gloom Fogarty recognized him. 'Ahiga!' he said.

The newcomer gazed intently at him as Fogarty put the gun back in its holster before approaching his old friend with his hand outstretched. As he came close the Navajo let out a low gasp.

'Fogarty!' he said. He grasped Fogarty's hand and they embraced. 'What on earth . . . ' he began and then decided to abandon whatever he had been about to say. Instead he put an arm round Fogarty's shoulder. 'It's good to see you,' he said.

'You're losing your touch,' Fogarty said. 'I heard you outside the hogan.'

'Guess I must be gettin' careless.'

There was no chance of getting any sleep that night. Ahiga set about making his friend something to eat. After that they went outside and sat together smoking and drinking thick black coffee mixed with forty-rod, exchanging stories. When Fogarty reached the point about the Wanted poster and told Ahiga his suspicions, the Indian grew excited.

'You're probably right about Goffin and his gang,' he said. 'They've been causin' trouble all around these parts for a while. Let me tell you what happened to me. Those varmints took my sheep and damn near killed me. I tracked the sheep to a box canyon. There's a whole heap of the critters there, not just mine.' Fogarty looked hard at his friend. 'A lot of people are gettin' plumb scared, but I aim to do somethin' about it,' the Navajo continued. 'I aim to get those sheep back — all of 'em.'

'Sounds to me like a little assistance could be welcome.'

'I hoped you'd say that. I got somethin' in mind. That's why I wasn't here when you arrived. I've been scoutin' things out. A place called Canyon del Fuego. That's where we'll find 'em.'

'Sounds good to me,' Fogarty said. 'In fact, it suits me fine. I didn't figure on makin' acquaintance with Goffin so soon.'

'You've got a day to rest up,' the Navajo replied. 'Make the most of it.'

* * *

Following an old wagon trail, they rode up to the Canyon del Fuego. Although it was early, the heat already bounced off the rocky walls. It was aptly named. Above them great slabs of stone hung above the trail, looking as though they might fall at any moment. They followed the track until they came to a cross canyon into which they turned their horses, following it for a couple of miles till they came to yet another narrow opening.

'This is it,' Ahiga said. 'It looks difficult but it soon opens out into a closed meadow. Just at the edge there's a grove of cottonwoods with a hogan the rustlers use.'

They spurred their horses on till they could hear the bleating of sheep and the occasional tinkling of a bell and soon saw the hogan standing at the edge of open grass where a large number of sheep and some goats were grazing.

'What now?' Fogarty enquired.

'Maybe it ain't much of a plan.' The Navajo grinned. 'But I figure we just ride in and start those sheep movin'. There's only one way they can go. We'll take those rustlin' varmints by surprise.'

'Good to see you've thought this through,' Fogarty remarked.

'Pull up your neckerchief. We don't want them to see who we are.' They checked their guns. 'Ready?' Ahiga asked.

Fogarty nodded. At a sign from the Navajo they applied their spurs and came charging out of the trees, shouting loudly. The startled sheep began to bleat and run in all directions before moving in panic towards the cottonwoods and the trail out of the canyon. One bunch split away and Ahiga veered round to herd them back again, swinging a lariat over their heads.

The doorway to the hogan broke open and three men emerged, looking confused. Drawing their guns, they began to fire. It was wild shooting and mainly served to stampede the frightened animals further. Two more figures emerged from behind a rock and commenced to blaze away with rifles. A shot flew over Fogarty's head and he swung round to return fire. The three men from the hogan were running towards them and he saw one of them reel backwards as a shot from the Navajo took him in the shoulder. The other two took shelter behind a tree and continued shooting. The noise was deafening as the gunfire echoed back from the cliff above them. The sheep were headed down the defile when yet another figure emerged from cover to loose off a couple of shots, which whined by uncomfortably close.

The sheep were well down the canyon now and as Ahiga followed them, still shouting and swinging his lariat, Fogarty turned to hold back any pursuit with his six-guns. Another shot ricocheted from rocks. Fogarty fired once more, then swung his horse to follow the flock. The sheep were slowed down now as the canyon narrowed and some of them were attempting to climb higher up the canyon walls. Fogarty feared disaster but he had not reckoned with the skills of his companion; although there were some casualties the main body of sheep was guided through the gap and into the broader canyon beyond.

Fogarty glanced back, expecting pursuit, but they had a good start on the rustlers. As they passed under the overhanging rocks Ahiga paused and, pointing up, began to fire. Fogarty took his hint and opened up with his Henry. The noise was tremendous and had its effect as first one and then another of the rocks began to sway and then, almost in slow motion, to topple down the side of the cliff.

Spurring their horses forward till they were well clear, Fogarty and the Navajo looked back as the rock fall came crashing down to the canyon floor.

Dust rose into the air and a horde of smaller stones came rattling down in the wake of the big boulders which now effectively blocked the canyon behind them. Ahiga grinned once more.

'I reckon it's going to take 'em some time to make their way past that,' he said, lowering his neckerchief.

'Was that part of your plan as well?' Fogarty retorted. They both laughed.

'Better get after those sheep,' Ahiga said. 'I know a place to keep them till we can get word to their owners.' Now that the excitement was over Fogarty became conscious again of the stifling heat in the canyon. They took swigs from their leather canteens and then followed the flock.

The afternoon sun was low in the sky when they got back to the hogan. When they had eaten they sat out again, smoking and talking things over.

'That was an enjoyable little escapade,' Fogarty said.

'It sure was, but it won't mean anythin' to the Ocotillo Kid.'

'His boys took a bloody nose.'

'That's all it was. This little sheep-rustlin' caper hardly signifies in Goffin's grand scheme of things.'

'Is that so? What else can you tell me about him?'

The Navajo paused and shrugged his shoulders. 'Where do I begin?' he replied. 'He and his gang started operatin' around these parts about six months ago, rustlin' sheep and cattle mainly. But that was just the start. Since then they've gone on to other things. If there's anythin' shady goin' on, you can be sure they'll be behind it.'

'It's quite a ride from Hackberry to here. Seems like they cover a lot of territory.'

'Sure. Once they got goin', they started to attract every outlaw and gunslinger lookin' for easy pickin's.' Ahiga turned to his friend. 'If you're thinkin' about goin' up against them, I guess you'd better know what it is you're gettin' into.'

Fogarty drew on his cigarette. 'Appreciate it,' he said.

'You and this man you figure they killed — what was his name?'

'Ben, Ben Arrowsmith.'

'You went back a long way?'

'Nope. But we got along.'

'So why did you leave?'

'I soon realized I'm no prospector. I figured if there was more gold in those streams, he was welcome to it.'

The Navajo nodded. 'Yeah, I know what you mean. Tell you the truth, I've been feelin' that way about herdin' sheep.'

'You just got your flock back.'

'I figure other folk could manage 'em better. Nope, I think a time's come for movin' on.'

'So what'll you do? You got a nice set-up here.'

'Maybe. At least till the Ocotillo Kid or his gang decide to wreck it.'

'You figure it'll come to that?'

'It will unless I do somethin' about it.'

Fogarty eyed the Indian closely and a smile began to play around the corners of his mouth. 'It might be real tough for one man to go against Goffin,' he said, 'but two . . . well, that would be a different matter.'

Ahiga grinned. 'There's another bottle of that Forty-rod back in the hogan,' he said. 'I reckon we should drink to the partnership.'

★   ★   ★

Marshal Shackleton had spent a good part of the night thinking about his prisoner's escape and had almost come to the decision that the affair wasn't really any of his business. The original incident had occurred at a place beyond his jurisdiction. If a man calling himself Vince Packard had not turned up claiming to be a witness, he wouldn't have known anything about it. Likewise, if Fogarty had not arrived in Hackberry, he wouldn't have become involved. Looking back on the affair, he had to admit that maybe he had been a little high-handed in his approach to Fogarty. Hell, it wasn't any of his concern. He had plenty of other things to worry about.

It was only when he got to his office early the next morning and saw the damage that he changed his mind. It was obvious what had happened; the missing guns were proof enough. He didn't like the feeling that to some extent it was his own fault. He should have taken the possibility of Fogarty's return into account. He had been careless and the thought of it rankled. Slamming the door behind him, he made his way to the Capitol Hotel. He wanted to have another word with Packard. It only took a few minutes for him to reach it. The desk clerk looked up somewhat nervously as he burst through the door.

'I'm lookin' for one of your guests,' the marshal said. 'A man called Vince Packard. Is he in the dining room?'

The clerk involuntarily glanced in

that direction although he knew that Packard wasn't there. 'Mr Packard left early this morning,' he said.

'He did what? Are you quite sure about that?'

'Yes. He was particularly anxious to reach Dry Fork in order to catch a train.'

'He gave me no indication that he intended movin' on.'

The clerk looked blank. 'I can only tell you what happened,' he said.

'What time was this?'

'Half past six. I had only just come on duty.'

The marshal blew out his cheeks and thought for a moment or two. 'Then he can't have got far,' he said.

Without waiting for a reply he turned and walked out through the door. He quickly made his way to his office where he took a bottle of bourbon out of a drawer and poured himself a stiff drink. The day had begun particularly badly and it didn't promise to improve when he looked out of the window to see his deputy approaching. He felt foolish. Somersby was little more than a boy and the marshal didn't like to feel that he wasn't setting him a good example. He tossed back his head, swallowed the whiskey, quickly put the cap back on the bottle and returned it to the drawer. The door opened and Somersby entered.

'Mornin', Marshal,' he said.

'Mornin'.'

Somersby suddenly noticed the broken window and the glass on the floor. His eyes swept up to the peg on the wall where the gunbelt had been hanging.

'Looks like Fogarty came back durin' the night,' the marshal said.

Somersby grimaced. 'Shouldn't we go after him?' he replied.

The marshal nodded. He no longer had much choice and besides, he didn't like the idea of anyone getting the better of him.

'Never mind about tryin' to put a posse together,' he said. 'That would only take more time. Let's you and me saddle up and ride out right now.'

2

Cora Siddons sat in a corner seat of the stagecoach and peered through the window at the dry, sun-bleached country outside. It was unfortunate in a way that the railroad line didn't extend further than Dry Fork, but she'd been in luck because a stage to Hackberry had come through on the same day she arrived and she hadn't needed to spend any time waiting around. She shifted uneasily. The leather of the seats was worn and cracked and she felt uncomfortable. The stage shook and jolted as it travelled along the rough, rutted track, rocking on its thorough-braces with every rise and dip of the terrain. Dust muffled the horses' hoofbeats and hung in a yellow pall outside the windows, obscuring the view.

She stole a glance at the other

passengers, trying to guess their occupations. There were three of them: a nattily dressed man of middle years who she guessed was some kind of drummer; another man dressed more casually, who looked as though he might be a stock buyer; and a younger man of somewhat rougher appearance she was unable to place. Her guesses were probably wide of the mark because she was new to the country. As her thoughts turned to what might await her in Hackberry, she couldn't help a certain frisson of apprehension.

Her reflections were interrupted when the stage suddenly began to slow. With a final lurch it came to a halt. She heard sounds of movement overhead, and then the door was pushed open and the driver leaned in.

'An obstruction on the road,' he said. 'It'll take us a few minutes to move it. Might as well take the chance to stretch your legs.'

With his assistance she climbed down. Ahead of them a tree lay across the track. The other passengers got out. The two older men joined the driver and the guard as they considered the best way to remove it. As she watched, four figures emerged from cover, all of them carrying rifles. They wore their bandannas pulled up to conceal their faces. Three of them looked pretty indistinguishable but she couldn't help but take notice of the fourth man, who appeared to be their leader. He was unusually long and thin. His companions were by no means small, but he towered over them.

'Drop your guns!' the tall man barked.

The stagecoach guard was taken unawares but he had taken his Winchester with him and instinctively he swung it up. Immediately two shots rang out and he spun backwards, blood pumping from his chest. He crashed to the ground and lay unmoving.

'I wouldn't try anythin' else if I were you,' the man said.

'I ain't carryin' no weapons,' one of

the passengers offered.

'Me neither,' the one who looked like a drummer said.

The younger man hesitated for a moment before unbuckling his gunbelt and throwing it to the ground.

'Frisk them,' the tall man snapped.

While his men carried out his commands Cora shrank back. She suddenly realized that the stage robbers hadn't noticed her. She began to tremble. Would any of the other passengers give her away? Scarcely daring to breathe, she kept on retreating till the looming bulk of the stage stood between her and the outlaws. There was plenty of cover to hand. Praying that their attention would be given to the other passengers, she slipped between some paloverde trees. Silently she kept on moving, expecting at any moment to hear the sound of footsteps behind her. She was in an arroyo. The ground was littered with old prickly-pear pads and spiny cholla segments and she almost let out a cry when a loose segment of cholla lodged itself in the back of her calf. She limped on till she found a narrow, precarious trail leading up a dry side gully and followed it till, worn out with the strain and exertion, she flung herself down in the shade of a sycamore. Then she heard the muffled sounds of gunshots.

★ ★ ★

Fogarty and Ahiga spent the next day at the hogan before starting out the following morning. Fogarty had been half-expecting a visit from the outlaws but Ahiga was confident that they would not be able to find the canyon. They rode up by a different trail from that along which Fogarty had made his approach and they were soon in the foothills. When they had ridden a little further Fogarty drew his horse to a halt and glanced back at the mountains. They seemed to float above the desert floor, ethereal and mysterious. The sky was vast and the air shimmered.

'It is a good land, is it not?' the Navajo said.

'It will be when we've cleared it of scum like the Ocotillo Kid.'

They rode on till Ahiga slowed his pinto and pointed to the heavens. High above them a few black dots hung in the blue void. 'Buzzards,' he said.

'They've probably spotted a deer carcass,' Fogarty replied.

The Navajo shrugged. 'Maybe, but somewhere in that direction is the stage route.'

'You figure we ought to take a look?'

'It ain't much out of our way.'

Fogarty gave a wry grin. It was true that they had no definite plan other than to make their way back to the spot where he and his partner had been prospecting. The heat was oppressive and they had been planning to rest up till the worst of it had passed; instead they set off in the new direction. After a time the trail they were riding intercepted a broader ribbon of track which wound through the rugged terrain like a snake. The road was pitted and scarred with wheel ruts and the unmistakable sign of horses.

'Looks like the stage from Dry Creek came through fairly recently,' Ahiga said.

Fogarty pondered his words for a moment. 'What's the next stop along the line?' he asked.

'Hackberry,' Ahiga replied. Fogarty had told him what had happened to him there but the Navajo didn't elaborate and only gave Fogarty a quizzical glance.

Neither of them had much chance to think about the matter because a bend in the trail suddenly brought them their first sight of the stagecoach. They drew their horses to a halt and reached for their rifles.

'Somethin's wrong,' Fogarty said. His eyes swept the rocky landscape. A palpable silence seemed to hang over the scene, broken only by the faint buzzing of flies.

'There isn't anybody around,' Ahiga replied. 'Nobody alive, that is.'

They rode forward and as they got closer they could see the obstacle in the road which had obviously caused the stage to halt. The stagecoach stood at a slight angle and the horses still stood in their traces. The bodies of the driver, the guard and the three passengers lay sprawled in the dust.

'The tree trunk must have been laid across deliberately,' Fogarty said.

The Indian turned from examining the corpses and moved to the side of the stagecoach. 'Look here,' he said. 'There are footprints leading away from the scene.'

Fogarty looked where Ahiga indicated but he could not discern anything. The Indian had moved to the rear of the coach. 'They lead into the woods,' he said. 'They are the footprints of a woman.'

Quickly they plunged into the trees. Again, Fogarty would have had no idea which way to go, but the Navajo picked his way unhesitatingly through the brush.

'Better go steady,' Fogarty said. 'If it's a woman passenger we don't want to frighten her.'

They followed the course of the arroyo till its junction with the narrow gully. When they turned off Fogarty could just make out the woman's tracks. They pressed on and soon they could see what they were looking for: a huddled shape in the shadow of a sycamore tree. The woman was obviously oblivious of their presence and for a moment Fogarty feared that she might be wounded or even dead. Just at that moment, however, she started and jerked upright.

'Don't be afraid,' Fogarty called. 'We are friends.'

In response she struggled to her feet but made no further movement as Fogarty and Ahiga emerged into the open.

'We were passin' by. We saw what happened to the stagecoach.'

Suddenly the woman swayed and would have fallen had Fogarty not rushed forward and caught her in his arms. 'It's all right,' he whispered. 'You're safe now.'

★   ★   ★

It was late at night. Between them, Fogarty and Ahiga had buried the victims of the Ocotillo Kid's attack on the stagecoach before setting up camp. They had tried to prevent the girl from seeing the bodies, but she had insisted on doing so.

'Why would anyone do something like this?' she asked.

Fogarty had no answer. The passengers had been robbed and the mailbag had been removed, but he knew that wasn't really an explanation. The girl had no appetite but Ahiga persuaded her to eat some of the beans and bread that he prepared. She drank coffee from a tin mug. When they had finished they made themselves comfortable. The stagecoach stood a little way beyond the circle of light thrown by the fire and

Fogarty was wondering what to do with it. The obvious thing would be to harness up the horses and drive it into Hackberry, but there were obvious problems with that idea.

'I hope you don't mind me askin', Miss Siddons,' he said, 'but I was wonderin' what brings you to these parts.'

'Of course I don't mind,' she replied. 'My uncle is the town marshal of Hackberry. Since my mother died, he's the only family I got left. He's alone in the world and so am I, so it seemed only sensible to come out and join him.'

At her words Fogarty started. 'You say the marshal is your uncle?' he said. Across the flickering flames his eyes met those of Ahiga.

'Yes. You seem a little startled. Is there something unusual in that?'

Fogarty recovered himself. 'Nope, not at all.'

'Do you by any chance know him?'

Fogarty was tempted to lie but something in Cora's open expression prevented him from doing so. 'I have come across him,' he replied.

'He's a good man. I've been looking forward to starting a new life out West.' She drank more coffee before speaking again. 'What will we do now?' she said.

'Well, I figure we ought to get you safely to your uncle. You can sit in the stage and we'll drive it the rest of the way.' A look of fear spread across her features.

'Don't worry,' Ahiga said. 'Those outlaw varmints won't strike again. They've got what they wanted. Besides, me and Fogarty can look after ourselves.'

'Have you any idea who was responsible for this?'

Fogarty hesitated, unsure about how much to tell the girl and not wanting to unsettle her. Again his eyes met those of Ahiga; the girl noticed and seemed to sense that something was being left unsaid.

'Is it true that you and Mr Ahiga discovered me by chance?' she asked.

Fogarty considered the matter briefly. It seemed to him that if he prevaricated he might only succeed in worrying the girl further. She was looking at him eagerly and he decided the best way was to tell her what he knew about the Ocotillo Kid.

When he had finished she looked at him with wide eyes. 'You mean that you and Ahiga are on the run from my uncle?' she said.

'Just me, not Ahiga,' Fogarty replied.

'But that is silly,' she said. 'I can see at once that you're not the sort of person who would harm anyone deliberately. I can't understand how my uncle could have made such a mistake.'

Fogarty didn't reply and they lapsed into silence for a while before she suddenly spoke again. 'You said that my uncle claimed that he had a witness. Whoever it was must have been quite persuasive. But that doesn't sound like the Ocotillo Kid's way of doing things.' She shuddered. 'Not from what you've told me and from what happened here.'

41

'How do you mean, ma'am?'

'Well, I don't see why he would have bothered to frame you. Surely shooting would have been more in his line.'

'She's got a point,' Ahiga said. 'Fact is, I been wonderin' some myself.'

Fogarty scratched his chin. 'Yeah,' he replied, 'I see what you mean.'

'Well, anyway, I certainly believe your story,' Cora said after a few moments. 'I know you couldn't have killed your partner, and when we get to Hackberry I'll make my uncle see sense as well.'

Fogarty laughed. 'Well,' he said, 'it sure is good to have you on my side. I guess if anybody can persuade the marshal, it's gotta be you.'

She was suddenly more serious. 'I don't want to get you into trouble,' she said. 'I can understand if — '

'Don't worry your head about me,' Fogarty interrupted. 'Just try and take it easy. We'll get you to Hackberry and then see what happens.'

She got to her feet. 'I'm feeling very tired now,' she said. 'I hope you don't mind if I turn in.'

'You could make yourself comfortable in the stagecoach,' Fogarty said.

She smiled and shook her head. 'No,' she replied. 'If it's OK with you and Mr Ahiga, I think I'll just settle right here.'

'Hope it ain't too rocky.'

'It will do just fine,' she answered.

She lay down a little way from the fire. After a time Ahiga rose also. 'I'll take watch,' he said. 'Why don't you get your head down too?'

'I'll do it,' Fogarty responded. 'I figure I might need to do some thinkin'.'

'About what happens when we get to Hackberry?'

'Yeah, that and a few other things,' Fogarty replied.

★ ★ ★

Mr Wes Baxter was the man to watch in Hackberry. In addition to a ranch called the Blister Beetle, he owned the Hungry Loop in town and he was just about to start a new business venture. To that end he had come to see Horace Stokes, the owner of the *Hackberry Epitaph*, and he entered the newspaper offices carrying a paper in his hand. A young man seated at a desk got up as he entered.

'Good day, Mr Baxter,' he said. 'Can I be of help?'

Baxter looked beyond him towards a room at the rear where the printing press stood. 'I want to see Stokes,' he said.

Just at that moment the man himself emerged. He was small and wore an apron over his trousers. He looked at Baxter through thick spectacles. 'Come through,' he said. He led the way to an inner office which was crammed with boxes full of papers and books piled untidily on top of each other. There was barely room for a desk and a couple of chairs.

'Well,' he said when they were both seated, 'what can I do for you?'

Baxter almost threw the paper he had

been holding onto the desk in front of Stokes, who glanced briefly at it but didn't bother to read it through.

'Can I leave that advertisement with you?' Baxter said.

'Sure. It'll be in the next edition.'

'It's about a new venture. My foreman, Taggart, suggested the idea to me, and I'm beginnin' to think it makes a lot of sense. Sheep farmin'. Just think it through. This is the place for longhorn sheep. People like to shoot 'em, but has anyone ever thought of breedin' 'em?'

Stokes reflected for a moment. 'The Navajo are good sheepherders,' he remarked, somewhat inconsequentially.

'Maybe so, but I got somethin' more in mind,' Baxter told him. He got to his feet. 'You could do worse than make a real front-page news story out of that notice,' he added, indicating the paper he had given the newspaperman. He went through the door to the outer office. The apprentice looked up.

'A pleasure doin' business with you,'

Baxter said. He opened the main door and stepped out onto the boardwalk where he stood for a few moments, allowing his gaze to wander up and down the street, his chest puffed out in a glow of satisfaction. Then he began to make his way towards the Hungry Loop.

When he came through the batwings the first thing he saw was his brother seated at a table with some of his friends. It wasn't hard to miss his tall, angular frame. Baxter didn't like any of them. It was true that the Ocotillo Kid and his gang had been quite useful to him in the past, but that time was gone. He had outgrown them. But having become embroiled with them, how was he to get out of it now? With a scowl on his face replacing his former expression, he walked across to their table and pulled out a chair.

'I thought I told you I didn't want you hangin' about the Hungry Loop,' he said.

'Now, that ain't the way to treat a

brother,' the Kid replied.

'If I hadn't sworn to Ma to look after you, I'd be happy to see you hang.'

The Kid glanced around. 'Don't talk too loud,' he said. 'Someone might get the wrong impression.'

'Why don't you clear out of town? There ain't nothin' for you here and you're puttin' us both at risk. Head back to the ranch. It's a lot safer that way.'

The Kid glanced towards the bar where a few of the girls were talking together. 'I figure we earned a little rest and recuperation,' he said.

'What have you been up to now?'

'Later,' the Kid said. 'Right now me and the boys got other things to attend to.'

Baxter's eyes followed those of his younger brother. 'Take your pick,' he said. 'Just don't cause any trouble and make sure you're gone before mornin'.' He got up and strode to the bar where the bartender acknowledged him deferentially.

'What can I get you, Mr Baxter?' he said.

'Nothin' for the moment.' He turned to the girls and said a few words to one of them. Then, without looking back, he made his way up the stairs. The room he used when he was in town was the last one at the end of the carpeted corridor. It was big and luxuriously furnished and a balcony overlooked the main street. He strode across the room and flung himself on the bed. His good mood had completely evaporated. His kid brother had seen to that. He was becoming more of a nuisance day by day. Something needed to be done, but what?

There had been a time when he had been able to control him, but now that the Kid was riding the hurricane of his own growing reputation he had become a threat and a liability. If some of the things he and the Kid had been involved in were ever to come to light, it could spell the end of all his ambitions. He needed to think of something, of some way out of the impasse in which he had become enmeshed.

He got to his feet, approached a drinks cabinet and poured himself a stiff bourbon. Then he cut and lit a big Havana cigar and, making himself comfortable in a leather armchair, set his mind to solve the problem.

★   ★   ★

Marshal Shackleton and his deputy drew rein on a long rock ledge beside a clear pool of water. Shackleton dropped from the saddle and bent down close to the ground while his deputy's eyes swept the surrounding country. Out in the cactus and creosote bush a flock of quail rose into the air.

'It's no good,' the marshal said, standing erect again. 'There are plenty of animal tracks and droppings: javelina, skunk, badger, but nothin' that could be assigned to Fogarty or anybody else, for that matter.'

'You reckon we've lost him?'

'It was only guesswork that got us this far. We could take a look around. It's the sort of place someone might use as a campsite, but there's no chance of us findin' anything.'

The deputy got down and they both looked about for indications of recent human occupation, but there was no trace.

'Might as well take a rest,' Shackleton said. They tethered the horses and then built smokes.

'What do we do now?' the deputy eventually asked.

Shackleton took a deep pull on his cigarette. 'I've been thinkin',' he said. 'Maybe we — maybe I — got this wrong.'

'How do you mean?'

The marshal hesitated. He didn't like to admit to the possibility of having been too hasty. Then he took the plunge.

'I think maybe I overreacted when I arrested Fogarty. Maybe I was a bit quick to accept what that *hombre* Packard had to say.'

'Remember, Fogarty resisted arrest,' Somersby replied. 'He managed to escape and then later he came back and trashed your office. That doesn't sound like the action of an innocent man to me.'

'Maybe not. Still, when you look at it, it's only Packard's word against Fogarty's. And when I called in at the Capitol Hotel to have another word with Packard, he'd already left.'

'He'd gone? Where to?'

'The hotel clerk said he'd checked out early to make his way to Dry Fork to catch a train.'

Somersby thought for a moment. 'We could head for Dry Fork; see if he turned up there.'

The marshal nodded. 'That's a possible option,' he said, 'but I don't think so. It's a bit strange he decided to leave so quickly, and somehow I don't think he'd want to advertise just where he intended goin'. I figure it's more likely to be a story to put anyone off his scent.'

'You reckon he might have been lyin' about Fogarty?'

'I don't know. Either way, I figure it ain't really our concern.' Shackleton got to his feet, flicked the stub of his cigarette to the ground and stamped on it with his boot heel. 'Come on, we've wasted enough time,' he said. 'Let's get on back to Hackberry.'

Without more ado they stepped into leather and began to ride. As they did so, the marshal was thinking that, despite what he had just said to Somersby, he would still like to meet up with the elusive Mr Packard. He felt somehow almost as if he had a stake in the affair. He didn't like unfinished business.

3

The marshal was looking out of the window of his office when he became aware that something was happening further down the street. Numbers of people were moving in that direction and he could hear a babble of voices. There was a general air of excitement. He rushed to the door and flung it open.

'Holy Moses!' he exclaimed. 'It's the stage at last! Somersby! Come with me!'

He began to run, fearful of what he might find. The stage had not arrived in Hackberry when it should have done. Cora hadn't stated exactly which stage she would be on, but the marshal had spent anxious hours worrying about her.

A large number of townsfolk had gathered outside the depot and a scene of confusion greeted him as he arrived. One glance at the stagecoach assured him there was nobody inside so he pushed his way through the little throng and into the building, where he came to an abrupt halt. Facing him was not only his niece but the man he had spent time looking for: Fogarty. Next to them both stood the depot clerk, looking ruffled and harassed. For a moment none of them said anything till Cora broke the spell.

'Uncle Clem!' she exclaimed. 'Oh, I'm so glad to see you.' She rushed forward into the marshal's grateful arms.

'Cora,' he said, 'Cora.' He looked over her shoulder at Fogarty as Somersby burst into the room behind him. He was feeling confused and it seemed to him that Fogarty must be implicated in what had happened to the stage. Disentangling himself from Cora's embrace, he reached for his gun as he approached his erstwhile adversary.

'I don't know what's goin' on,' he

said, 'but you ain't gonna get away this time.'

Fogarty made no move to defend himself and when the man standing next to him made a move to draw his gun, he placed a hand on his arm.

'Uncle!' Cora cried. 'Put that weapon down. This is Mr Fogarty and Mr Ahiga. They rescued me after the stage was set upon by outlaws.'

The marshal turned back to her, more confused than ever, at which point the depot manager intervened.

'It's true,' he said. 'Apparently the stagecoach was ambushed by a gang of desperados. They killed the other passengers as well as the driver and the guard. Without the intervention of these two gentlemen, the lady might not have survived.'

Shackleton stood irresolute, looking from one person to the other for further enlightenment.

'For what it's worth,' Fogarty said, 'I didn't kill anybody.'

The marshal looked at him closely

and then put his gun back in its holster. 'No,' he said, 'I guess you probably didn't.' He swung round to face the press of people behind him. 'OK, folks,' he said. 'The show's over. There's nothin' more to be done at the moment. I suggest you get on about your affairs.'

Most of the folks turned and began to move away. A few still hesitated and someone shouted: 'What are you gonna do about this?'

The comment seemed to sting the young deputy because he turned and, approaching the speaker, said: 'I'll tell you what we're gonna do. We're gonna catch whoever's responsible for holdin' up the stage and make sure they pay for what they done. In fact, if you feel so strongly about it, you can be the first to offer yourself to be deputized when we start out after the varmints.'

The man's tongue flickered out and he licked his lips. 'That won't be necessary,' he mumbled. 'I didn't mean to imply anythin'. Besides, I got business to attend to.'

He turned and walked quickly away. His departure was the signal for the rest of the crowd to disperse. When they had gone the deputy's face wore a somewhat shamefaced expression. 'Sorry,' he said, 'I suppose I just took exception to the man's attitude.'

The marshal grinned. 'Well, I guess you made that pretty clear.'

Cora's gaze was directed at the deputy. 'I think you were quite right,' she said. 'It wasn't just what he said. It was his whole attitude.'

Regarding them both, Fogarty thought he detected a tinge of red appear on the deputy's cheeks.

'Just so long as he don't go antagonizin' too many of the good citizens of Hackberry,' Shackleton remarked. He turned to Fogarty and Ahiga. 'It seems I got a lot to be thankful to you for. I figure we need to do some talkin'.'

* * *

The Blister Beetle ranch lay torpid in the blistering heat of the afternoon sun when the Ocotillo Kid and his bunch of outlaw companions arrived back after their night in town. After leaving their horses in the corral, the gunslicks made their way to the bunkhouse while the Kid entered the main building.

'Hello! Anyone at home?' he shouted.

He had seen no sign of his brother's horse so the silence only confirmed that he hadn't got back yet. The Kid grinned. Wes might express disapproval of his behaviour from time to time, but he was probably doing the same thing as he had been doing the night before. He poured himself a drink and slouched back on the settee, putting his feet up on a low table. He knew what his brother would say about that. The thought galled him and he deliberately scraped his boot-heels across its surface. Hell, he reflected, his brother owed his position to the things he had done for him in the past. What about that sheep-rustling caper, for

58

example? He didn't understand what his brother was up to, but it had been a lot of fun. It was only recently that Wes had started to raise objections, but he had no intention of reining in his behaviour.

Since getting out of jail and hitting the owlhoot trail again, he had been enjoying himself. It was good to be back with the boys and raising Cain. His brother was good cover. Although he had various places of retreat throughout the area, the ranch was the best base. And, of course, there were the manifold advantages offered by the Hungry Loop. Yes, it was a pretty good set-up, and he didn't intend to let anything spoil it.

* * *

Fogarty hadn't given a lot of credence to Cora's confident assurances that she could persuade her uncle of his innocence, but he had seen little alternative to returning the young lady and the stagecoach to Hackberry. He was even more surprised, therefore, when the marshal invited him and Ahiga as well as his deputy to supper that evening. In fact, it was Cora who had hinted at it, but Shackleton seemed more than happy to oblige. Cora was keen to try her cooking on her uncle but Ahiga, who took some pride in his own culinary skills, persuaded her to let him help. Somehow, Somersby succeeded in insinuating himself into the team as well. The result was a very palatable and satisfying meal, after which they all sat out on the veranda of the marshal's house to enjoy coffee and the cool of the evening.

'I'd like to say again how grateful I am to you and Ahiga for coming to Cora's rescue,' the marshal said to Fogarty.

'It was nothin',' Fogarty replied. 'It was just lucky that we came by when we did. Ahiga found her tracks.'

'I don't know what might have happened to me otherwise,' Cora said.

'Don't think any more of it,' Fogarty said.

'So, Ahiga, you were sayin' that the Ocotillo Kid was responsible for runnin' off your sheep?' Shackleton continued.

'Yeah. We got 'em back, though.'

'Can you be certain it was him? He seems to cover a lot of territory.'

'It was him, or some of his boys,' the Navajo replied.

'Just like it was almost certainly him who carried out the stage massacres,' Fogarty said.

'And you figure he's the man responsible for killin' your partner? That's somethin' else I owe you for. I shouldn't have jumped to conclusions. I shouldn't have swallowed that story Packard told me.'

'Don't worry about it,' Fogarty replied. 'Anyway, I ain't so sure that it was the Kid any more.'

'We were talking about it after Mr Fogarty and Ahiga found me,' Cora interposed. 'It seemed to me that stopping by Hackberry in order to invent a story and frame Mr Fogarty for a murder he didn't commit isn't the way this man — the Ocotillo Kid — would go about things.'

'The Kid could still have done it,' the marshal said.

Somersby had been quiet so far. Glancing at him from time to time, Fogarty was aware that his attention was focused on Cora. Now Somersby took advantage of a pause in the conversation to make his voice heard.

'There's one way we might be able to flush out whoever was responsible,' he said. The others turned to him.

'Yes? What would that be?' the marshal said.

'Well, he doesn't know that Mr Fogarty is free. If he did know, he surely wouldn't be very pleased. I mean, having gone out of his way and taken all that effort to set him up. So, if he realized that his plan hadn't succeeded, might he not try to remedy the situation?'

Fogarty thought for a moment. 'I

reckon you got somethin' there,' he said. 'Yes, you've definitely got a good point. If Packard could somehow be made aware that his plan had failed, there's a good chance he might try somethin' else.'

Cora looked anxious. 'But wouldn't that be placing you in a position of some danger?' she said.

'Cora's right,' the marshal said. 'Fogarty, you'd be settin' yourself for a clay pigeon.'

'Maybe so,' Fogarty replied, 'but I figure I can take care of myself.' He turned to Somersby. 'Thanks for that,' he said. 'I figured my next step was to find Packard, but it would have been just about impossible. This way, I can let him come to me.'

'How are you goin' to do that?' Ahiga said.

Fogarty turned to the marshal. 'Is there a newspaper in town?' he asked.

'Sure. The *Hackberry Epitaph*. It's owned and operated by a man called Horace Stokes.'

'Good. One thing we can do is put somethin' in the newspaper, some sort of story that would make the reader aware that I was still around.'

'Ain't it a slim chance that Packard would read it? He's probably long gone now,' Ahiga said.

'You could be right. On the other hand, I got a notion that he's still somewhere close.'

'It seems like a long shot to me.'

'What have I got to lose? If he takes the bait, then we're in business. If he doesn't, I'm no worse off.'

'I don't like it,' the marshal remarked.

'Neither do I,' said Cora. 'It's too dangerous. I think it would be better just to leave things alone.'

Fogarty leaned towards her. 'Don't worry about me,' he said. 'Like I say, I can take care of myself. I swore to find out who killed my partner. I can't let it rest till I've done that and brought the varmint to justice.'

'Well, whatever happens,' the marshal said, 'you got my support.'

'The same goes for you,' Fogarty replied. 'It don't take much savvy to know the Ocotillo Kid ain't gonna rest on his laurels. There won't be any real peace till he's back behind bars.'

The marshal turned to his niece. 'I'm sorry you had to run into all this,' he said. 'Are you sure you don't just want to turn right around and catch the first train back East?'

She smiled and placed her hand on his arm. 'You are a silly,' she said, glancing at Somersby as she did so. 'This is my home now. I don't want to be anywhere else.'

*   *   *

Wes Baxter, aware that his brother and his no-good gang would be likely to spend a few days at the ranch, decided to stay in town. He had all the comforts he could want at the Hungry Loop and besides, there were matters to attend to connected with his plans for the Blister Beetle. He could rely on his foreman,

Taggart, to keep an eye on things. Taggart had been with him a long time. He could trust him. Baxter had spent a restless night thinking about his brother and what he should do about him. He was making his way towards the bank when a sudden thought struck him. Why bother about trying to arrange a loan when he could get the Ocotillo Kid to carry out a robbery? Even better if it wasn't the Hackberry bank that was the target, but the bank in Dry Creek, which conducted business on a bigger scale. If, in the course of doing so, his brother should be seriously injured or killed, well, that would be just too bad.

He had no doubts that the Kid would welcome the idea. He would only be giving fate a little tip in the right direction. His brother knew what risks he was taking. He got a positive kick out of placing himself in danger. Let things take their course. If he got rid of the burden of his brother, it wouldn't be his fault. If the Kid got away with it, they would both benefit.

The only thing that worried him was the possibility that the Kid might give him away, but that was something he faced anyway. If his brother spilled the beans, he would simply deny it. The Kid had no proof of his involvement. No one would believe him. No one would believe the word of a killer and robber over that of a respectable citizen, a pillar of the community and, moreover, a man about to bring even more prosperity to the town.

The more he thought about it, the better he liked it, and it was with a spring in his step that he passed the bank and entered the barber shop instead. Although he didn't really need one, a decent trim would set him even more aright with the world.

★   ★   ★

It didn't take Cora Simmons long to adjust to life in Hackberry. Back East she had been just another commonplace young woman with nothing to mark her out. Here, she felt more significant; a strange glamour attached to living on the frontier and to being the niece of the town marshal. Hackberry suited her and she enjoyed walking its streets, calling in to the shops and stores and making the acquaintance of the other citizens. Her arrival was a topic of interest for a little time, and she enjoyed that too, added to which there was all the excitement of discovering a new country.

On the afternoon of the second day after her arrival the marshal came back early. There was a smile on his face and even before he spoke Cora sensed that he was concealing something.

'How are things?' she queried.

'Fine. Fogarty called by earlier. He's put something in the *Epitaph* about offerin' a reward for information about the killing of Ben Arrowsmith. That should stir up some interest from Packard, whoever he is.'

A worried expression clouded Cora's features. 'I still don't think it's a good idea,' she said. 'I'd rather Mr Fogarty just forgot about trying to find this man Packard.'

'I don't know about that, but I figure he didn't even need to place anything in the paper. If it isn't already evident to Packard that Fogarty is a free man, it soon will be. Fogarty isn't exactly makin' himself scarce. I guess that's part of the plan.'

'He's taking unnecessary risks.'

The marshal approached her and placed his hands on her shoulders. 'Leave Mr Fogarty to worry about all that,' he said. 'I'm sure he knows what he's doin'.'

She looked up at him and her expression cleared. 'I suppose you're right,' she said.

'Yes, you'll see. And now I want you to forget about Mr Fogarty and come with me.'

'Why? Where are we going?'

'Not far. No, not that way. Out the back door.'

Taking her hand, he led her through

the back entrance into the garden which sloped gently down to a corral screened by some trees. As they got closer she saw that there was a horse in the corral.

'There,' Shackleton said. 'He's yours.'

She hesitated for a moment, then with a muffled cry she ran forward. The horse was looking over the top rail of the corral and she patted its head.

'It's mine?' she said. 'Do you mean . . .'

'Yes. I bought it today from Mack Hordern at the livery stables. He tells me he's a good one, but I figure you can see that for yourself.' The horse was a roan gelding quarter horse, stocky and well-muscled. Cora leaned down and tore up some grass to feed him with.

'He's lovely,' she said, 'Say, can I ride him now?'

Shackleton chuckled. 'I figured you'd want to do that,' he said, 'so I got a new saddle too. Here it comes now.'

He turned back towards the bunk-house and, following his lead, Cora saw

Somersby coming towards them, carrying something across his shoulder.

'Howdy,' Shackleton called. The deputy came up, looking a little embarrassed.

'Why don't you help Cora saddle him up?' Shackleton said.

Somersby looked uncertainly at the girl.

'That would be nice,' she said.

'When you've done that, Somersby will take you for a ride. Just till you get to know your way around. I know you can ride perfectly well.'

'Are you sure you don't mind?' Cora asked the deputy.

'Of course he doesn't mind!' Shackleton exclaimed. 'You don't mind, do you, Somersby?' The deputy marshal mumbled something in reply as Cora turned to her uncle and began to thank him.

'Don't bother with any of that now,' he replied. 'Go on, you're wastin' time. Go easy on him till you get to know him better.' He paused and grinned. 'The horse, I mean.' Without waiting for any further response, he began to walk back towards the house. Cora watched him for a moment before turning to Somersby.

'Where's your horse?' she said.

'Waitin' in the stable,' he replied.

'Come on, then, help me get this saddle on.'

It didn't take them long. The saddle was different from anything she was accustomed to. It was bigger, with a low cantle and a rounded horn, and made of prime leather. When the horse was ready she swung into the saddle; it felt strange but already comfortable. She waited for a moment, talking gently to the horse, till Somersby rode up alongside her. Somersby seemed more assured once he was on horseback. He took the lead as they both rode out towards the open country. Their way took them through a grey-green arid landscape of creosote bush and iron-weed. They rode for a considerable time in silence before Somersby eventually brought his horse to a halt. Cora drew rein beside him.

'This wasn't my idea,' Somersby said.

'I didn't think it was. I understand that my uncle put you in charge of me.'

'It wasn't exactly like that, but it was certainly his idea.'

'Well, since we've got this far and I for one am enjoying the ride, it seems to have been a good one.'

Somersby hesitated. 'Do you mean what you say?' he asked. 'I'm sorry. That probably doesn't sound quite as I intended it. I mean, are you sure you don't mind being forced to have me along?'

'I wouldn't have seen it in those terms,' Cora replied. 'But no, I don't mind at all. Not, that is, unless you do.'

Somersby shook his head. 'Of course not,' he replied. 'In fact, I'm really enjoying it too.'

Cora shielded her eyes against the sun. 'It's a wonderful country,' she said. 'It's not like anything I've seen before. It's wild and desolate, but it's very beautiful.'

Without replying, he dug into his saddlebags and pulled out a pair of field-glasses which he put to his eyes before handing them to Cora.

'Over there,' he said. 'A herd of bighorn sheep.'

Cora took a long look through the glasses. She counted eight of them, browsing on the brush. One big ram carried massive horns which curled in a magnificent spiral.

'It's not usual to see them round here,' Somersby said. 'They usually prefer higher ground.' Cora handed back the glasses and he replaced them. He looked up at the sky. 'Maybe we'd better be startin' back,' he said.

'Just a little further,' Cora replied. When they rode on, they did so side by side.

The heat of the day was subsiding and Cora was enjoying the feel of the breeze on her face. The whole terrain was new and exciting to her and she drew attention from time to time to some of the features of the landscape; a group of ocotillo cactus waving their spidery arms, the high, fluted column of a saguaro. Somersby was enjoying himself too. The awkwardness he had previously felt in Cora's presence had vanished but he was torn between his desire to continue the ride and a growing concern that they should turn back. It was Cora herself who made the decision. Coming to a halt, she stood upright in the stirrups, staring about her.

'I'm so glad you're here,' she said. 'I think it would be very easy to get lost.'

'Just so long as you remember a few basic rules,' Somersby replied. Cora waited, expecting him to say more, but he didn't bother to elaborate.

'You'll have to tell me what they are when we get back,' she said. Somersby liked that comment. It seemed to imply some continuity to their time together. 'I guess we'd better do that now. After all, I don't want to get you in trouble with my uncle.' She chuckled and he grinned sheepishly.

'I wouldn't want that to happen,' he replied.

She looked at him closely. 'How long have you been my uncle's deputy?' she asked.

'Not long. About six months, I guess.'

'What were you doing before that?' She coloured slightly. 'I'm sorry; it's really none of my business.'

'I was workin' in the general store, but it was boring. I've known Mr Shackleton one way or another for quite a long time. I got talkin' with him about it one time. I asked him if I could become a deputy marshal. To be honest, he wasn't too sure about it at first.'

'Were you born in Hackberry?'

'Nope. I was born and raised in Phoenix. My old man is still there. We didn't always get on too well.'

'Isn't there an element of danger to the job?' she asked. 'Does that not worry you?'

'Well, you might not believe it after all that's happened recently, but really

Hackberry is a pretty quiet sort of place. Nothin' much usually happens apart from the odd drunk kickin' up a stir, that sort of thing. In fact, I don't think Mr Shackleton had much need for a deputy. I reckon he was doin' me a favour.'

'Well, I'm sure you're returning it by doing a very good job,' she replied. She smiled at him and then stroked her horse's mane. 'I think he's had a pretty good work-out, don't you? Come on, we'd better be starting back.'

'Have you thought of a name for him?' he enquired inconsequentially.

'No, but I should, shouldn't I? Have you any suggestions?' Once again her words encouraged and gratified the deputy marshal. 'No doubt we'll think of something between us,' she added.

*　*　*

Fogarty and Ahiga had installed themselves in the town's only hotel, the Capitol, but it didn't take the Navajo long to decide that it wasn't for him. At breakfast he announced his intention of checking out. Fogarty knew there was no point in wasting time arguing with him.

'I need to stay,' he said. 'I need to make myself conspicuous.'

'Yes,' Ahiga replied. 'It is all part of drawing Packard to you.'

'We need a rendezvous, some place where I know I can find you.'

'There is a dry stream bed a few miles out of town. It's called Jackrabbit Draw. I'll wait there.'

'It could take some time.'

'I'm not goin' anywhere. Not till you've dealt with Packard and we've both dealt with the Ocotillo Kid.'

'You think there is a connection?'

The Navajo shrugged. 'Everything is connected,' he replied.

He got up and walked out of the room. Fogarty watched his retreating figure till it was out of sight and then poured himself another cup of coffee. He glanced around, observing the other guests. There was a well-built woman of middle years, a younger man who Fogarty guessed was some kind of drummer, and a family group comprising a man, a woman and two youngsters of about eight and ten. The man looked a lot older than the woman and the kids were well behaved.

Shackleton had given him a brief description of Packard, but it didn't amount to much. The man had worn his hat pulled low and, despite his training, the marshal had not paid him a lot of attention. Neither of these two men could be him. Besides, Packard had checked out of the hotel. It was unlikely, given the circumstances, that he would return.

Fogarty finished his coffee, got to his feet and walked out of the dining room. As he passed the desk he paused and approached the clerk. 'Mind if I take a look at the register?' he said.

'Help yourself,' the man replied, pointing to the book. Fogarty opened its covers and riffled through till he found the page on which the name *Packard* was inscribed in a barely legible scrawl. Had he deliberately written it that way? Or was that his genuine style? Maybe he wasn't very literate? Maybe Packard wasn't his real name anyway? But as he looked at it, it seemed to Fogarty that he had seen something like it before. He thought hard for a moment before giving up. No, it could be anybody's handwriting. There was nothing to be deduced from it.

'Can you remember anythin' about the man who wrote this?' he asked.

The desk clerk took a glance. 'No, I'm afraid not,' he replied. 'I think the night clerk must have been on duty when he signed in. I do recall him leaving early.'

'What did he look like?'

The man thought for a moment before shaking his head. 'I'm sorry,' he said. 'I really didn't take much notice. I had only just come on duty and had other things to attend to.'

'Was he tall, short, fat, thin?'

The clerk's brows puckered. 'I really couldn't say,' he replied. 'I guess he was just kinda average.'

A mundane, run-of-the-mill sort of character with nothing to distinguish him from the mass. Marshal Shackleton had barely noticed him either. It was almost as if he didn't exist, or only as a phantom.

'Thanks anyway,' Fogarty said. 'If you do remember anythin', I'd appreciate it if you could let me know.'

'Marshal Shackleton and the other man said the same thing,' the clerk replied. 'If you don't mind me saying so, folks seem to be payin' this Packard *hombre* a considerable amount of attention.'

Fogarty had been about to walk away, but the clerk's words jolted him back to attention. 'The other man?' he said. 'What other man?'

'Well, not long after the marshal came . . . '

'You mean, the same day Packard left?'

'Yes. The marshal had gone too on some business. Anyway, another man came and asked to see Packard.'

'Did he say why?'

'No, and I didn't think it was any of my business to ask him. I simply told him Mr Packard had left. He just turned round and walked away.'

'Did he seem surprised?'

'No. Like I say, when I told him Mr Packard had left, he just turned and left.'

'Can you recall what he looked like?'

The clerk's brow wrinkled briefly in thought. 'There was something,' he said. 'I don't know that I would have thought anything of it if you hadn't asked.'

'Well, what was it?'

'It wasn't anything much. It was just that, when he looked at me, one of his eyes seemed to be lookin' somewhere else.'

'You mean he had a cast in his eye?'

'Yes, I guess that was it.'

'Thanks,' Fogarty said. 'I really appreciate your help.' He turned and walked quickly away. When he was outside the hotel he carried on walking, thinking over what the clerk had told him. A man with a cast in his eye. One of the other prospectors had had an eye like that. What was his name? He struggled to remember for a few moments. Yes, Henderson. They had spoken a few times. There had been an incident when he had rescued an old-timer from the river and Henderson had helped him drag the oldster up the riverbank. It didn't have to mean anything. There could be lots of people with minor eye defects. Still, it was something of a coincidence. Especially now that he also remembered where he might have seen that spidery writing of Packard's before. Ben Arrowsmith wrote that way. So, probably, did any number of other people. Again, it didn't have to mean anything. But if it did, what did that tell him about his former partner? He might have discovered some clues, but he felt more in the dark than ever.

4

When Wes Baxter finally got back to the Blister Beetle, he had his plans pretty well laid. As he expected, when he came through the door it was to find the ranch house in a state of general disrepair. Chairs had been overturned, glasses lay about most of the surfaces, and there was mud on the carpet and the furniture. His eyes noticed immediately where the Kid's boots had scraped his favourite table. Normally he would have got angry, but his temper was assuaged now that he had a definite purpose in mind. Checking to see if his brother was there, he found the rooms upstairs in a similar state. He looked out of a window; one of the ranch hands was passing by and he called out to him: 'Have you seen my brother?'

'He rode out with a few others earlier. I think they were goin' huntin'.'

He turned away and went back down the stairs. Hanging on the wall was the head of a pronghorn antelope. He liked hunting himself, but for his brother it was neither a sport nor a skill: just an opportunity for wanton slaughter. And the Kid made little distinction between animals and people. Again Baxter felt troubled about the prospects of being incriminated in the Kid's activities. Too many people already knew about their relationship. If it became general knowledge that his brother and the Ocotillo Kid were one and the same person, things could get really awkward. He felt confident about being able to ride out any difficulties, but his anxiety only served to strengthen his resolve. He walked across to his liquor cabinet. It was severely depleted. He poured himself a stiff whiskey and went outside to sit on the veranda and wait for the Kid's return.

★ ★ ★

It was dark as Fogarty approached Jackrabbit Draw. He had been thinking over what the hotel clerk had told him but he was no nearer a solution to the mystery. He needed to get a second opinion, and he had decided to talk it over with the Navajo. Besides, he tended to grow restless if he spent too long with a roof over his head, and the prospect of a night in the open appealed to him.

Even before he got there he sensed that something was wrong. He had expected to see an indication of his friend's campfire but there was only blackness. Ahiga was adept at concealing his presence but he still felt uncomfortable. He rode into the draw, his horse's hoofs making no sound in the dust, before swinging down from the saddle. Taking his Henry rifle, he crept forward on foot.

The place was eerily quiet. There was no moon but the stars cast a ghostly light, enough for his keen eyes to detect the marks made by two horses. They had ridden in from an angle and then followed the dry stream bed. They looked quite fresh. Quickening his pace, he pushed forward. Thrusting through a thin screen of brittlebrush, he emerged into a patch of open ground and saw a sprawling figure which he knew was that of his friend. Forgetting caution, he rushed forward and knelt down beside him. His fingers touched something wet but Ahiga was breathing and in a moment his eyes opened.

'Fogarty!' he muttered.

'What happened?' Fogarty asked.

'Two men jumped me. You'll find one of 'em dead somewhere close, I reckon. The other one got away.' Fogarty looked at his hand. Blood smeared his fingers. 'I'll be OK,' Ahiga said. 'I took a slug in the thigh but I don't reckon it's serious.'

'Just take it easy,' Fogarty replied, 'while I take a look.'

Bending close, he examined the Navajo's injury. It seemed that Ahiga was right. The bullet had torn through the flesh and Ahiga had lost a considerable amount of blood, but it wasn't as bad as Fogarty had feared. He quickly undid his necktie and fastened it round Ahiga's leg as a tourniquet.

'You're sure there ain't any more of the varmints around?' he asked.

Ahiga shook his head. 'There were only the two of 'em.'

'In that case, just give me a few minutes to get my horse. I've got medicines in the saddlebags.'

He slipped away and returned leading the horse. He took a small bag and a flask and knelt down again beside Ahiga.

'This is gonna hurt,' he said. 'Take a swig or two of this. It might help.' The Indian didn't need a second invitation. He tipped the flask up and swallowed. Afterwards, Fogarty did his best to clean and dress the wound. Ahiga handed the flask back to him and when he put it to his mouth, there was only a trickle.

'Thanks.' The Navajo grinned. 'I

never felt a thing.'

Fogarty knew differently but he only grinned back. He glanced around. 'I'll just take a look,' he said, 'and then you can tell me what happened. By the way, where's your horse?'

'They must have turned it loose. I guess it can't be too far away.'

Making sure his friend was comfortable, Fogarty slipped away into the surrounding shadows. It didn't take him long to find the dead man. He was lying on his back with his face turned towards the heavens. He had been shot twice. As soon as Fogarty saw him he knew who he was. Somehow, he didn't even feel surprised. The pieces of the puzzle just seemed to fit. He left the body, and after walking a short distance he found both the man's horse and Ahiga's pinto. He led them back to where he had left the Navajo.

'I figure we could both do with some warmth and some hot black coffee,' he said. Ahiga made to struggle to his feet but Fogarty gently restrained him. 'You don't want to set off the bleedin' again,' he said. 'Like I say, you just take it easy. I'll soon have us cosy as a rattlesnake down a gopher hole.'

When he had built the fire and prepared the coffee with water from his canteen, he sat down next to Ahiga and produced his pack of Bull Durham. They built smokes and made themselves comfortable.

'How's that wound?' Fogarty said.

'It hurts but you done a good job on it.'

'So what happened?'

'They came on me out of nowhere, but they bungled it. I was lucky. I just had enough time to roll away and get off a shot. When he realized his friend was hit, the other one just rode away. He obviously didn't have the stomach for facin' up to me alone even though I was hurt.'

'You only fired one shot?'

'Yeah. Anythin' strange in that?'

Fogarty hesitated before shaking his head. 'Nope. I just figure you were a

mite careless to let them get that close.'
They both inhaled deeply and Fogarty
topped up their coffee mugs.

'Anyway,' Ahiga said, 'what brought
you out here?'

'Well, I came to try and work out
some answers to a few questions, but I
guess I already got them.' Ahiga gave
Fogarty a puzzled look. Fogarty wasn't
sure where to begin but, after taking
another long drag on the cigarette, he
gave Ahiga a brief account of his
conversation with the hotel clerk. 'I
couldn't make sense of what he was
tellin' me,' he concluded, 'at least, not
till now.'

'What do you mean?' Ahiga said.

'That *hombre* you shot; I recognized
him.' Ahiga, forgetting his injury for a
moment, attempted to sit up but sank
back with a wince.

'Steady,' Fogarty said.

'So who was it?'

'I could be wrong, but I'm pretty
sure it was the man I told you about,
the one with the cast in his eye who was

prospectin' near to me and Arrowsmith. He's called Henderson.'

'Hell, that's some coincidence.'

'I figure it's no coincidence,' Fogarty replied. 'I reckon he and Arrowsmith must have seen us together and tracked you out here. They obviously came with the intention of killin' you. And if I'm right, it means that the other man who got away is my ex-partner.'

Ahiga still looked puzzled. 'I'm not sure I understand you,' he said.

'It kinda confirms what I was beginnin' to think already. Arrowsmith betrayed me. I had a stake in that claim and he must have realized there was gold to be found. The irony is that I really wasn't interested in it. He couldn't understand that. He musta figured I'd be back. So he concocted the story of his own death and then tried to pin the blame for it on me. Tell me, can you remember what kinda horse that varmint was ridin'?'

'I couldn't be sure. Looked like it might have been a grulla.'

'Arrowsmith rode a grulla. That's one more link in the chain.'

'So you mean Arrowsmith ain't dead? That the whole thing was just a cockamamie story to get you out of the way?'

'That's the only way I can figure it. Maybe I'm wrong. I kinda hope that I am. But can you come up with a better explanation?'

The Navajo breathed deeply. 'Hell, it's a lot to take in. Are you sure you ain't jumpin' to conclusions?'

'Well, there's one way of provin' it,' Fogarty replied.

'What's that?'

'Find Arrowsmith. If I'm right, Arrowsmith and Packard are one and the same person. And we got witnesses who can identify Packard. He might not have made much of an impression on either the hotel clerk or the marshal, but I figure they'll recognize him when they come face to face.'

Ahiga thought about Fogarty's comments for a few moments. 'If that's the case,' he said, 'I guess it means Arrowsmith must have taken the bait of the article you put out in the *Hackberry Epitaph*.'

'Yeah. I feel kinda sorry about it now. If it weren't for that, you probably wouldn't have ended up gettin' shot.'

The Navajo shrugged. 'Flushin' out the varmint was the whole point of the exercise. You've no cause to blame yourself.'

Fogarty inhaled deeply and then blew out a jet of smoke. 'If Arrowsmith is the one who shot you,' he said, 'then he can't be too far ahead.' He stopped and his gaze dropped to the Navajo's damaged leg.

'Don't worry about me,' Ahiga said. 'I'll be fine by the mornin'.'

'We'll see,' Fogarty replied. He knew that the Indian's wound was too severe for him to travel far.

'You go on anyway,' Ahiga said.

'There'll be plenty of time to get on Arrowsmith's trail,' Fogarty replied.

'The longer you leave it the less

chance you'll have of catchin' up with him.'

'It ain't but a short distance back to town,' Fogarty replied. 'You need to see a doc.' He looked at the Navajo and grinned. 'You might have to come to terms with stayin' at the hotel for a night or two, though.' The Indian grunted. 'Still, they do a real good breakfast,' Fogarty added.

★   ★   ★

Marshal Shackleton was standing in the doorway of his office looking down the main street as Somersby approached. He was walking in a sprightly fashion and he raised his hat to one old lady as their paths crossed.

'Things seem kinda calm, don't they?' the deputy said.

The marshal nodded and replied with a curt 'Yeah.' The scene was certainly peaceful. Some of the women-folk were out shopping; at one corner three elderly men stood talking together and a buggy was drawn up outside the grocery store with a dog sitting in it. Somersby stood next to the marshal, observing the scene, before giving him a closer look. The marshal's face looked tired and drawn.

'You look worried,' Somersby said. 'Has somethin' happened?'

'Well, that's one thing I can't accuse you of,' Shackleton replied. 'In fact, you seem to have somethin' of a spring in your step.'

'It's a lovely day,' Somersby replied. 'Why not?'

The marshal looked down at him and his expression softened. 'Come inside,' he said. 'There's somethin' I need to tell you.' He led the way into the office and they both sat down.

'What is it?' Somersby said.

'I had a visit from Fogarty.'

'Fogarty?'

'Yeah. It's a bit of a long story.' In as few words as possible, he told the deputy marshal about what had happened to Ahiga and of Arrowsmith's role.

'Is Ahiga OK?' Somersby asked when he had finished.

'He will be. I've arranged for him to be taken to my house. Cora can help look after him.'

'So Packard never existed? It was just a name Arrowsmith was usin'?'

'Seems that way. After everythin' Arrowsmith's done, not forgettin' makin' me look a fool, I'd sure like to get my hands on him.'

'Fogarty's gone searchin' for the varmint?'

'Yeah, and now I come to think it over, I figure I might just take a ride myself. The way Arrowsmith seems to operate, Fogarty might need a hand.' He thought for a moment, looking at Somersby. 'You wouldn't mind takin' care of things for a spell?' he asked.

'Sure. You don't need to worry about anythin'.'

'It shouldn't take long. Maybe I'm worryin' about nothin'. After all, Fogarty can take care of himself. I just got a feelin', that's all.'

'No problem. You get on and do what you need to do, and I'll look after things till you get back.'

Shackleton moved towards the door, then paused. 'Don't go talkin' to Cora,' he said. 'I don't want to get her worried just as she's settlin' in. Oh, and by the way, thanks for takin' her ridin' and showin' her round. I sure appreciate it.'

Somersby suddenly felt awkward. 'Always glad to be of help,' he said.

Shackleton opened the door, looked back once again, and then stepped out into the sunlight.

* * *

After leaving Ahiga Fogarty rode back to Jackrabbit Creek. It didn't take him long to find the tracks left by Arrowsmith, but after a time they became more difficult to follow. He could have done with having the Navajo alongside him. The traces left by Arrowsmith's horse grew fainter and were overlaid with deer tracks and others which he figured were made by javelinas. He slowed the horse to a walking pace, studying the tracks as he went and stopping now and then to dismount and take a closer look.

After a time he dipped down into another draw and unexpectedly came upon the remains of a camp-fire. There were some coffee grounds nearby. Clearly, Arrowsmith had felt sufficiently secure to stop. Fogarty thought about it. Arrowsmith had probably fled from the scene of the shooting in something of a panic, but once he had got away he had probably reflected that there was little danger of pursuit since the Indian had clearly been wounded. The faded imprints of a shod horse were like those that he had picked up at Ahiga's camp. Arrowsmith was probably not far ahead. After examining the sign, Fogarty got to his feet, stepped into the leather and rode on.

He had come prepared, if necessary, for a long ride, so it came as something of a surprise when he realized that the

99

tracks he was following had disappeared. He drew to a halt and then retraced his steps. He hadn't gone far when he found the tracks again. They turned away quite abruptly, following what looked like an old, faded trail through the brush. He sat his horse, turning the matter over. Why the abrupt change of direction? Could Arrowsmith have become aware that he was being trailed? He didn't see how that could be. It could only mean that Arrowsmith had a specific destination in mind, and somewhere not so far from Hackberry as he had imagined. Where could it be?

Suddenly Fogarty remembered that, although the country was arid and wild, there were still some ranches in the area. Could Arrowsmith be making for one of them? Touching his spurs to the horse's flanks, he turned off up the new trail. Sure enough, the sign continued in that direction. He rode through a stand of pecan and mesquite trees, then suddenly drew rein. Ahead of him, in a patch of meadow, stood a one-room shack with a pole corral behind it. Although he had seen no sign of any cattle, it bore every resemblance to a line camp. It seemed he was already on ranch land. There was a horse in the corral, but it wasn't a grulla.

He dismounted and after tying his horse to a tree crept forward on foot. By circling the shack he was able to remain in cover but he could not get close except by crossing the patch of open ground. He inched forward, cradling his rifle, till he reached the corral. He was anxious not to alarm the horse and he whispered to it, trying to pacify it. He looked towards the shack. There was no rear window and he decided to take his chances.

Breaking cover and bent almost double, he ran swiftly forward, not stopping till he had reached the shelter of the cabin wall. He pressed close to it, straining to detect any noises from inside. Hearing nothing, he edged forward again till he came to a corner of the building. Crouched low, he slipped round the angle till he was beneath the window. It was partly open but there was still no sound.

He decided to take the bull by the horns. Shuffling past the window, he reached the door and stood upright. He took a few moments to gather himself and then kicked hard at the door. It flew open and he burst through the opening, his rifle at the ready. In an instant his eyes had taken in the scene. The room was empty. Even as he registered the fact he felt a blinding pain at the back of his head and he pitched forward onto the hard earth floor. He heard a footstep behind him and his head seemed almost to explode again as darkness enveloped him like a heavy blanket.

*   *   *

It was the Ocotillo Kid's motto never to trust anybody, and least of all his brother. He was not unaware of his brother's ambiguous attitude towards him. So when Baxter broached the subject of staging a bank robbery, his enthusiasm for the idea was tempered by caution. Something told him to be careful. He and his gang had carried out many unlawful activities at Baxter's behest, from which they had both benefited. But Baxter hadn't come up with something quite as bold nor quite so close to home.

It was this thought which persuaded the Kid of the course he should follow. Sure, it would be a lot of fun to rob a bank, but he decided on something different. According to what his brother had told him, a big shipment of bullion was due to arrive by train for the bank in Dry Fork. He didn't question how Baxter had come by the information. He obviously had contacts. The arrival of the railroad had put that town on the map, and business was thriving. The bank was much bigger than the one in Hackberry and it needed funds. It made sense.

However, instead of waiting for the

money to be transferred from the train to the bank, why not attack the train itself? That way, if his brother was playing him false at all, he would foil him. No doubt the train would be guarded, but to the Ocotillo Kid it still seemed a better proposition.

★ ★ ★

Fogarty came round with an aching skull and a throat as dry as an old prickly pear pad. He put his hand to his head; there was a bandage wrapped round it. The room was dark but even as he struggled to make things out the door suddenly opened. A large figure was framed in the doorway. Despite his grogginess and the dim light, he could see that it wasn't Arrowsmith. He was taken aback, however, when the man spoke.

'Fogarty, you old devil. I thought I heard you stirrin'.'

'Shackleton! What the hell are you doin' here?'

The marshal entered and came close. 'Sorry about buffaloin' you,' he said. 'I figured you must be that varmint Arrowsmith.'

Wincing with pain, Fogarty slowly eased his feet to the floor and sat on the edge of the bunk on which he had been lying. He put his head in his hands.

'I did my best to patch you up,' Shackleton said. Fogarty looked up at him and attempted a faint grin. 'I got some coffee on the boil. You just take it easy and I'll go get a mug.'

He shuffled away and while he was gone Fogarty succeeded in getting to his feet. His head felt like a herd of buffalo had stampeded through it. He made his way to the door. The marshal turned round at his approach. 'Are you OK? Take a seat. The coffee's ready.'

He came across and they sat together at the table on which a kerosene lamp shed a muted glow. Shackleton produced a flask.

'This might help the healin' process,' he said. He poured some of the contents into Fogarty's mug. Fogarty felt in his pocket and produced his pouch of Bull Durham. He rolled a cigarette and then handed the pouch to Shackleton. By the time he had taken a few drags and downed some of the coffee, he had begun to feel slightly better.

'Hell,' he said, 'you might have mistaken me for Arrowsmith, but did you have to whack me so hard?'

'Coulda been worse,' the marshal replied. 'I coulda shot you.'

Again Fogarty gave a wry grin. 'I don't understand any of this,' he said. 'Perhaps you'd better tell me what you're doin' here.'

'After speakin' to you, I kinda got to thinkin'. I figured you might need some help so I came after you. By the way, Ahiga ain't stayin' at the hotel. He's at my place. I figured he might be more comfortable that way and Cora is keepin' an eye on him. He told us what happened.'

'You came after me?'

'That was the idea; I figured you might need a hand. I came across sign and followed it here. I know your horse so I figured it was probably Arrowsmith's and that you might not be far behind. I pushed on ahead. When I saw the line cabin, I figured that was where Arrowsmith was headin'. When you bust through that door, I thought it must be him.'

Fogarty took a couple of drags on his cigarette. 'I trailed Arrowsmith right up to the cabin,' he said. 'We should be able to pick up his sign again.'

'You're not in any shape to go trailin' after anybody just at the moment.'

'I'll be all right soon enough.' Fogarty suddenly became conscious of the dark. 'How long have I been out of it?' he asked.

'Not long. It took me a while to clean up your wound. Apologies, but I ain't no doc. A few hours, I guess.'

Fogarty made to stand up but sat back again as his head began to pound. 'The longer I wait, the better chance he has of gettin' away.'

The marshal glanced out of the window. 'There wouldn't be any chance of pickin' up his trail in the dark,' he said. 'Better wait and see how you feel in the mornin'.'

Although he was anxious to be on Arrowmsith's trail, Fogarty could see the sense in Shackleton's suggestion. He drank more coffee before turning back to the marshal. 'One thing puzzles me,' he said.

'Yeah? What?'

'I figured Arrowsmith would try to make a clean getaway, but he didn't. He turned off the trail he was followin' to reach this place. It seems like he deliberately headed this way, as if he knew the shack existed.'

'Then why did he ride on?'

'I don't know. He must have got nervous. Maybe he picked up on the fact that one or even both of us were right behind him.'

The marshal reflected for a moment. 'This shack is on the Blister Beetle property,' he said. 'If he knew about it, it could be because he rode for the outfit at some stage.'

'That could be true. He told me he'd been doin' some ranchin' before decidin' to try his luck prospectin'. He said that workin' as a ranch hand was for fools. He figured to make his fortune a different way. I guess that was pretty much how I felt.'

'Were you makin' anythin' from that claim?'

'Not that I could see. Maybe he knew somethin' I didn't.'

The marshal thought for a few moments. 'Assumin' he's not comin' back here, where else would he be likely to go?'

Fogarty shook his head. 'It doesn't matter,' he replied. 'All I got to do is get on his trail. I'll catch up with him eventually.' He got to his feet and walked to the door. Opening it, he gazed out at the luminous landscape. 'I reckon that cool night air does my head some good,' he said.

The marshal joined him. 'You're determined to be off early in the mornin'?' he enquired.

'Sure. I'm feelin' a lot better already.'

'Then I'll be comin' too.'

Fogarty glanced at him and once again a grin lifted the corners of his mouth. 'I figured it that way,' he said. 'I reckon that's probably why you put Somersby in charge of things till you get back to Hackberry.'

'I never said anythin' about Somersby,' the marshal replied.

'You didn't have to. Somersby's a good man. The place will be in safe hands. Besides, I figure it won't take long till we catch up with Arrowsmith.'

5

The railway tracks glinted in the heat of the sun. Alongside them rode a bunch of riders led by the Ocotillo Kid, looking for the best spot to set up an ambush. The air shimmered and flies hung over their heads in clouds. The Kid peered ahead. He was looking for a place where the train would have to slow and where he and his men could remain concealed. The tracks began to climb a long gradient and then, up ahead, they took a curve near a grove of saguaros. It was the best spot he had seen and when they had reached it he ordered his men to stop and dismount.

'OK, boys,' he snapped. 'You know what you got to do.'

'The train ain't due yet,' one of the men grumbled.

The Kid turned on him, his face contorted with rage. It had not been an easy ride; he was hot and out of temper. 'Are you stupid or somethin'?' he hissed. 'Maybe you think I am?'

The man flinched. 'I was just meanin',' he began, but he stopped when the Kid drew his six-gun and waved it menacingly in front of him.

'Instead of mouthin' off,' the Kid said, 'maybe you should start loosenin' that rail.'

'Sure boss,' the man replied.

The Kid glanced at the others. 'Somebody'd better help him', he said. 'And by the way, watch what you're doin' with that dynamite.'

While his men were working at drawing the spikes, he sat in the shade of a saguaro and drank whiskey from a hip flask.

* * *

Somersby was doing some paperwork when the door of the marshal's office opened and Cora entered. She looked excited. She halted for a moment, as if she had expected to see not just Somersby but her uncle as well.

'The marshal's had to go off on some business,' Somersby said, noticing her hesitation. 'He's not sure just when he'll be back, so in the meantime he's put me in charge.' He was hoping for a sign of approval, but Cora seemed not to notice. He wasn't disappointed because her next words showed that it was not her uncle she had come to see, but him.

'I hope you don't mind me dropping in, but I was passing by and I couldn't wait to tell you. I've thought of a name for the horse,' she said. 'I've decided to call him Cholla.' Somersby wasn't sure what to say. 'Maybe you think it's silly,' she continued. 'I know it isn't the sort of name somebody would normally call a horse, but to me it sounds just right. Apparently it was standing on some cholla needles that made my foot sore, but now I associate the name of the plant with Hackberry. I'd never heard of it before. And besides, if I hadn't come to be with my uncle, I'd never have been given him.' She stopped and looked at Somersby. Something in her words made them both feel that more had been said than lay on the surface.

'I don't think it's a silly name,' Somersby said. 'In fact, just the opposite.'

She dropped her gaze and turned towards the door. 'I'd better be going,' she said. 'There are lots of things I have to do.'

Somersby got to his feet and accompanied her outside. 'Why don't we have another ride soon to celebrate?' he suggested.

'Yes, that would be nice,' she replied. 'I'll look forward to it.'

She began to walk away and he watched her as she crossed the street, but she didn't look back.

* * *

Ben Arrowsmith was no fool, and after the debacle at Jackrabbit Creek he knew that Fogarty would be on his trail. The ambush had been Henderson's idea. It hadn't worked out the way either of them had anticipated, but he had seized the opportunity it presented to get Henderson off his back. When he had ridden away from Jackrabbit Creek his one idea had been to get as far away as possible, but he soon had second thoughts. That would be the very thing Fogarty would expect him to do. He knew from the article in the *Hackberry Epitaph* that his plan to frame his ex-partner had failed. He also realized that Fogarty had probably placed the article in order to try and flush him out.

Then he reflected that the Blister Beetle wasn't far away. He knew the place well from the days he had worked there, and he figured that the old line cabin would make a good place to hide away till things blew over. No one would find him there.

He was taken by surprise to find a horse already in the corral. It was the last thing he had expected. He had to think quickly. Was it Fogarty's horse? Had Fogarty somehow already anticipated him? Maybe it was just a coincidence. One of the ranch hands might have simply put up there for the night. But he didn't like that explanation.

He decided not to take a chance. He bypassed the cabin and rode on in the direction of the Blister Beetle. It seemed to him a sensible idea to seek shelter there and merge in with the other work-hands. Baxter would remember him. And if he didn't, he had a story to tell which would certainly interest him and put him on his side. It would mean sacrificing some of his own interests, but it had become clear to him that he would probably need some assistance anyway to realize his dream. It was one thing that he knew about the disused silver mine; it was another thing to exploit that knowledge. Opening up the old mineshaft and setting up a proper apparatus for excavating the silver it contained would call for some proper organization. If there was as much silver to be found as he believed, there would be plenty for both him and Baxter. Maybe he had made a mistake not reasoning that way before he decided to set up Fogarty. In any event, he needed now to cut his losses.

★　★　★

When Baxter saw his brother ride out with a group of his closest desperados, he figured that something was afoot. Maybe the Kid had decided to go ahead and rob the bank. On the other hand he could just be setting off on another of his madcap escapades. He wasn't disappointed to be rid of him for a while either way. It made quite a change to be free of him.

As he sat on the veranda, a drink by his side and a cigar between his fingers, his reverie was disturbed when he saw a horseman appear. He watched him as he came steadily on. The rider came through the yard and drew to a halt. A couple of men appeared from the bunkhouse as he shielded his eyes against the sun to glance up at the stranger. The man looked vaguely familiar.

'You better have a good reason to come anywhere near the Blister Beetle,' Baxter said.

'I sure have. You won't regret hearin' me out.'

Baxter signalled for him to dismount before turning to his two ranch hands. 'Take his horse to the stable and then stay around,' he said.

At a nod from Baxter the man stepped up to the veranda and sat in a chair next to him. Baxter took a drink, looking closely at the newcomer as he did so. 'Don't I recognize you from somewhere?' he said.

'I reckon so,' the man replied. 'The name's Arrowsmith, Ben Arrowsmith. I used to work for you.'

Baxter thought he recognized the man now. If he hadn't left on his own account, he would have sacked him for being lazy. 'I remember you,' he said.

'Didn't you decide to go away and try somethin' else? So what are you doin' back here?'

Arrowsmith had been pondering the question of just how much to reveal to Baxter. In the end he had decided to say nothing of the Fogarty affair and concentrate instead on the mining angle. He knew enough of Baxter to realize that it was probably his best chance of staying safe.

'You're right, Mr Baxter,' he said. 'I went off to do some prospectin'. In fact, that's the reason I'm back here.'

Baxter's eyebrows lifted and the expression on his face convinced Arrowsmith that he was doing the sensible thing in telling him about the mine.

'I worked for a time along the Senita River. It was hard goin' and I didn't seem to be havin' any luck. Then things began to change. The gold I managed to wash out was kinda light in colour. I got talkin' with an old-timer. He told me that was because it was alloyed with silver. He figured there was plenty just waitin' to be dug out, a whole lode of it. I didn't believe a word the oldster was sayin' till he took me to a tunnel entrance in the hillside and told me he had helped dig it himself one time.'

He had Baxter's interest. The ranch owner leaned forward. 'Go on,' he said.

'Well, the long and the short of it is that this old-timer claimed to have found silver there. He wasn't interested in stayin' on to get any more of it. He reckoned he didn't have the time or the inclination to take it on any further. But if someone was prepared to make the effort, there was plenty more to be had.'

Baxter grunted. 'And you believed him?'

'I know it sounds unlikely, but I believed him because he showed me the beginning of the seam in the rock. He also gave me this.'

Arrowsmith reached into his jacket pocket and produced a piece of blue-black rock about the size of an egg. Baxter took it and hefted it in his hand. 'Why would he tell you all this?' he said.

Arrowsmith shrugged. 'Guess he wanted to hand on what he'd found. He was too old to care about strikin' it really rich any more. Besides, I did him a favour. I pulled him out of the water when he was likely to have drowned.'

The story was partly true. What difference did it make if it had been Fogarty who rescued him? In the end it was he to whom the oldster had passed on his information in gratitude, after Fogarty had left. He wasn't going to pass it on to anyone else. Arrowsmith had made sure of that. It was the oldster's body he had shown Shackleton to frame Fogarty.

'This don't look like silver,' Baxter said.

'That's what was left when he got the gold out. It's silver all right. Like I said, seems like the silver and gold is kinda mixed together.'

Baxter looked closely at the piece of rock. 'I don't know,' he said. 'Maybe you're right. But it ain't a lot to go on. Anyway, why are you tellin' me this?'

'I just figured you'd be interested. If there's any truth in the story, and there's silver to be found, one man on his own ain't gonna be able to do much. But in partnership with someone like you, Mr Baxter, someone with a bit of clout, well, maybe they could both make themselves rich. At the very least, it oughta be worth takin' a look.'

Under other circumstances Baxter would probably not have given the idea any more thought. But the way he was fixed, being short of money and increasingly desperate to find ways of financing his enterprises, it was a different proposition. It could be one more avenue. It could even be the answer to all his problems. Like the man said: at the very least it might be worth taking a look. He had heard stories and rumours of lost treasure in the desert mountains. It wasn't so long since news of gold on the Gila River had drawn hundreds of fortune-seekers to that area. The lucky ones had found gold in riverbeds or in surface gravel. Mining for silver was more complicated; ore had to be hacked out of rock and then processed. It would certainly take a whole lot more effort than an oldster would be likely to summon.

It was lucky that Arrowsmith had arrived with his story at a time when the Ocotillo Kid was away. The Kid didn't need to know about it. It appealed to Baxter's sense of irony that the Kid could be staging a bank robbery partly on his behalf while he himself was investigating a fresh source of wealth. Yes, it would certainly do no harm to consider the matter in more detail. In fact, the more he thought about it, the more it seemed important to act and not delay. Swallowing the last of his drink, he got to his feet.

'Find yourself a berth in the bunkhouse for tonight,' he said. 'Tomorrow you and I have got some ridin' to do.'

He turned to go indoors. For a moment Arrowsmith hesitated, waiting for him to return the block of silver, but he didn't. As the door closed on Baxter, Arrowsmith made his way down the steps and across the yard.

★　★　★

It soon became apparent to Fogarty and the marshal that Arrowsmith was aiming for the ranch house.

'What do you figure he's up to?' Fogarty asked.

'He obviously knows Baxter. We gathered that much from the fact that he knew about the line shack. From what I know about Baxter, I doubt whether he'd be welcomed with open arms.'

Fogarty thought for a moment or two. 'Unless he was able to offer Baxter somethin',' he replied.

They were riding slowly, on the alert for any signs of Baxter's men. They knew they couldn't be far from the ranch house and were wondering what course of action they should follow when they came on something which set their thoughts off in an entirely different direction. It was the clear sign left, not by Arrowsmith or any single horseman, but by a large bunch of riders clearly coming from the direction of the Blister Beetle. They slipped from their horses to look more closely.

'There must have been at least half a dozen riders,' Fogarty said.

'More, I reckon. Now what could they be up to?'

'Does it have to signify anythin'?' Fogarty replied.

The marshal stood looking about with his head slightly raised, almost as if he was sniffing the wind. 'Nope, I guess it don't have to,' he said. 'But then again, what kind of business could a bunch of riders this big be on? Hell, Baxter don't even graze anythin' on the Blister Beetle. Apparently he's talking about introducin' sheep, but at the moment the place doesn't support anythin' at all. Come to think of it, why would he be employin' as many people as he does?'

'Maybe he's brought in some men to start lookin' after the sheep.'

The marshal grinned wryly. 'Maybe, maybe,' he said. 'But I got a feelin' there's somethin' more to it. In fact, I don't like any of this at all.'

Fogarty suddenly slapped his thigh. 'Say,' he said, 'you don't reckon it could be the Ocotillo Kid and some of his owlhoots?'

The marshal gave him a sharp look. 'Why do you say that?'

'Why, we know the Ocotillo Kid is around. We know he's been causin' trouble; look at what happened to the stagecoach. You've been half-expectin' him to show up in Hackberry. Now we find this trail left by a whole bunch of riders. It could be him. Which way is the trail leadin'?'

'It ain't goin' towards Hackberry,' the marshal said. 'Looks like it's headin' more in the direction of Dry Fork.'

He paused, still looking about him. He took off his Stetson and scratched

126

his head. 'You know, you could have a point,' he said. 'And even if you're wrong and it's nothin' to do with the Ocotillo Kid, it still seems mighty suspicious to me.'

'So what do we do now?'

The marshal took a moment to consider the question before replying. 'The Ocotillo Kid isn't your concern,' he said.

'He is after what happened to Cora and the folk on that stage,' Fogarty replied.

He was making some quick calculations. 'We're almost at the ranch,' he said. 'We might as well carry on for the moment. If Arrowsmith is there, all well and good. If he's not, then at least we'll know. Either way we won't lose much time till we're on the Ocotillo Kid's trail.'

The marshal regarded him steadily. 'It's my duty to deal with the Ocotillo Kid,' he replied. 'That's why I got a badge pinned to my chest.'

'Like I just said, I got a stake in

catchin' him too. Give me a little time to check out Arrowsmith. Then we can both go after the Ocotillo Kid. I figure an extra gun wouldn't come amiss.'

The marshal mused. 'I haven't forgotten what that Arrowsmith varmint did to Ahiga,' he said. 'I'd sure like to catch up with him. Trouble is: if he's there and I arrest him, I got to take him back to Hackberry. That's gonna take some time.'

'Leave Arrowsmith to me,' Fogarty replied. The marshal looked unconvinced but then he nodded. 'Then it's settled,' Fogarty said. 'First Arrowsmith, and then the Ocotillo Kid.'

He turned and was about to step into leather when the marshal halted him. 'Wait a minute,' he said. 'Seems to me like you might need to exercise some caution.'

'What do you mean?'

'If Arrowsmith is at the Blister Beetle, we don't want to advertise the fact that we're comin' on after him. And I've already said that I don't trust

Baxter. I'm surprised we've got this far without some of his boys showin' up.'

'Yeah, I see what you mean,' Fogarty replied. He put his hand up to his head on which a large bump had developed. 'I wouldn't want to make the same kind of mistake as last time,' he added ruefully.

The marshal grinned. 'And I've just thought of somethin' else,' he said. 'If those tracks were made by the Ocotillo Kid and some of his gang, then what were they doin' on Blister Beetle property?'

'I guess they musta just been passin' through.'

'I suppose so, but maybe there's somethin' more to it. The Kid don't usually show himself except when he's carryin' out one of his crimes.' The marshal looked up at the sky. 'It's gettin' pretty late,' he said. 'Let's wait till dark before doin' anythin' further.'

Fogarty was keen to press on but he could see the sense of what the marshal was saying. Besides, if Arrowsmith had sought sanctuary at the Blister Beetle, he wouldn't be going anywhere else in a hurry. 'I could do with a smoke,' he said.

The marshal pointed to some bushes. 'We'll rest up there. Nobody would be likely to see us. And I got somethin' here in my saddlebags will go nicely with that pouch of tobacco.'

* * *

The Iron Horse was making good time as it snaked across the dry desert landscape, rattling and rolling along the track. The engineer, his face and hands blackened and stained, leaned out to look ahead, and the brakeman, riding on top of the train, was poised to leap from car to car in order to apply the handbrakes when they should be required. Smoke and ashes blew back in a dense black cloud from the huge, bulbous funnel and drifted into the cars.

Inside, the passengers slumped back

in their seats and contended, not very successfully, with the heat and dust. Some of them attempted to pass the time by playing card games or reading. A few of them looked through the windows at the shimmering landscape. One of them was a lady of middle years wearing a voluminous blue calico dress.

The train was approaching a bend when the door at one end of the car opened and the train boy appeared, carrying a tray on which were candy, peanuts and cigars. The lady in blue calico turned away from the window to look up at him as he advanced down the aisle.

'Excuse me, young man,' she said, 'but I wonder: is the dining car open? If so, could you could direct me to it?'

He looked back at her but he didn't seem to register what she said. He looked agitated and his eyes flickered.

'I'm sorry,' she began, but didn't get any further because the train suddenly lurched and the train boy involuntarily staggered backwards. There was a loud noise and some of the people began to scream. The carriage seemed to rise into the air and then it came down to earth again with a sickening, grating shock. A number of people were lying in the aisle where they had been thrown. The lady looked towards the train boy and was surprised to see a gun in his hand.

'Young man,' she started to say, when the gun exploded. She was conscious of a searing pain in her shoulder. She looked down to see a dark stain spreading across the front of her dress. The shooting drew out more screams and shouts from the frightened passengers, then there was total confusion.

Although the Ocotillo Kid and his men had set the derailment themselves, it still came as something of a surprise to see the effects of their workmanship. The train had been moving quite slowly and it seemed to take a long time to leave the tracks. The engineer had been looking out of the cab and, as the engine began to topple, turning partly over, he was flung from it. The cars behind buckled and separated. The noise was deafening. Steam hissed and boiled and sparks flew as the wheels slid before leaving the track. The outlaws were gaping open-mouthed when the voice of the Kid brought them to their senses.

'Come on!' he yelled. 'Follow me!'

Above the din, the crackle of gunfire could be heard. Shots rang out from inside some of the coaches but the Kid wasn't surprised. He had already placed some of his men on the train. He ran alongside till he had almost reached the car containing the safe when a couple of shots rang past his head. He had a glimpse of a guard inside the wagon. Coming to a halt, he reached inside his jacket for the stick of dynamite he was carrying, lit it and hurled it through the cab door. There was a blinding flash of light and an explosion which sent shards of wood flying into the air and almost knocked the Kid off his feet. There were footsteps behind him as he was joined by some of his gunnies.

'OK,' he said. 'Let's just grab whatever's in there and then get out of here.'

They climbed into the shattered wagon. Through the smoke and dust the Kid could see two bodies sprawling grotesquely among the debris. The safe was lying nearby, together with a number of bags.

'Man, this is heavy,' one of the gunnies said as he tried to move the safe. With the assistance of one of the others, he succeeded in lifting it.

'Grab those bags!' the Kid ordered.

Further shooting was coming from some of the derailed carriages. The Kid looked through the door as two men appeared carrying rifles. A shot rang out from somewhere to their rear and one of them flung up his arms before falling headlong to the ground. The Kid pointed his six-gun and fired at the second man. He went down too.

'Time we got out of here!' the Kid exclaimed.

They jumped down from the train

and he shouted for the others to get back to the horses. Dense black smoke billowing from one of the other carriages provided cover for the outlaws and it took only a matter of moments for them to reach their mounts. They swung into leather. For a few seconds the Kid's eyes took in the chaotic scene. He was grinning inanely.

'Come on, let's ride!' he heard a voice call. Raising his gun to take a few final shots, he dug his spurs into his horse's flanks and wheeled away.

* * *

Darkness had fallen when Fogarty set off on foot to cover the remaining distance to the Blister Beetle. It had proved a sensible choice to seek cover: horsemen had passed close by on two occasions. There didn't have to be anything sinister in that, but it was prudent not to take unnecessary risks. With quick steps he padded across the dusty range, looking about him for any further riders.

The sky was huge and full of stars; clumps of cactus showed like gaunt, ragged fugitives against the horizon.

Eventually the dark mass of the ranch house loomed up out of the darkness. Light showed dimly in the curtained windows of the main room and in the bunkhouse behind. He crept by the side of the building, aiming for the stables. The door was open and he slipped inside. Horses stamped and snorted as he passed by the stalls, looking for Arrowsmith's grulla. In a few moments he found it. He grinned. *Looks like we were right*, he said to himself.

Before he could do anything else, the darkness was suddenly illuminated by a ray of light and a voice snapped: 'Don't move. We got you covered.'

For a moment Fogarty considered drawing his gun, but a bustle of activity behind him persuaded him that he was outnumbered.

'Put your hands in the air!'

He did as he was told and the next moment found himself surrounded by a group of men with six-shooters in their hands. A couple of them carried lanterns. By their glow he could see that the men were not ordinary ranch hands. There was no mistaking the look of hardened gunmen. In a moment he was forcefully seized; his arms were held behind his back in a vicelike grip while his own weapons were removed.

'Whatever you think, you got this all wrong,' he said.

By way of reply one of the men hit him hard in the stomach. He doubled over, retching, as someone shouted; 'Give it to him, Robardes!' There were shouts and whoops from the others.

'We caught you red-handed,' the man addressed as Robardes said. 'Now, horse-stealin' is a mighty serious offence.' He turned to the others. 'What do you say, boys? I figure hangin's the penalty for horse-theft.'

'String him up!' some of the men replied. 'Stretch his neck!'

There were more shouts and whistles; Fogarty could see that things were quickly getting out of hand.

'Perhaps Mr Baxter might have somethin' to say about that,' he said. For a few moments the merriment continued and then a gradual hush descended. Fogarty couldn't help but notice that Robardes hesitated before replying.

'Mr Baxter ain't here,' he said. 'He's left his foreman in charge.' He seemed to be weighing up the situation. It certainly seemed that Fogarty's reference to Baxter had unsettled him. In a moment he appeared to recover his swagger. He turned to his companions. 'OK, we'll take him to see Taggart and then string him up.'

The hoots of laughter began again as Fogarty was pushed forward. He had recovered his breath and instinctively he tried to break free. A swinging blow from Robardes this time caught him square on the jaw and sent him staggering backwards.

'That was mighty stupid!' Robardes snapped. Fogarty's arms were locked even more firmly behind him.

'That's enough!' Robardes barked.
The sudden activity had caused another
ripple of excitement but it quickly died
down as Fogarty was led out of the
stable to the front of the ranch house.
As they approached, the door opened
and a figure appeared silhouetted
against the light.

'What in hell's goin' on?' he snapped.
'I've told you boys before about causin'
trouble.'

'We ain't causin' no trouble,' Robardes
replied. 'We found this varmint snoopin'
around the barn. Seems like he wants to
see Mr Baxter. I told him he wasn't
around. We figured you'd be interested
in knowin' just what he's up to.'

The man leaned forward, trying to
make out the captive figure. 'Bring him
inside,' he said. Fogarty was dragged up
the porch steps to the veranda and then
unceremoniously pushed inside and
onto a chair.

'Robardes, you stay. The rest of you
get on back to the bunkhouse,' Taggart
ordered.

The men shuffled away and Robardes took up a position behind Fogarty while Taggart sat on a chair facing him. Fogarty had taken the opportunity to look around him. The room was comfortably furnished but for some reason bore the marks of wear. He wasn't particularly interested in the decor, however. He was looking for Arrowsmith but there was no sign of him. He looked at Taggart. The man was lean, gnarled and weather-worn.

'OK,' Taggart said. 'Perhaps you'd better explain what you're doin' on Blister Beetle property.'

Fogarty felt battered and bruised from the beating he had received at the hands of Robardes, but he had his wits about him. He remembered something Shackleton had said and the impression made on him by the men who had accosted him in the barn. He had a sudden intuition and he wanted to see what effect his words might have on Taggart.

'I'm lookin' for the Ocotillo Kid,' he replied.

He was watching Taggart closely and he wasn't disappointed; although Taggart remained stony-faced, it was clear to Fogarty that his words had caused a reaction.

'I think you'd better explain yourself,' Taggart said.

'There's nothin' to explain,' Fogarty replied. 'I was ridin' and I came on some sign. A lot of riders had been passin' through. I figured they might have been causin' some trouble to the Blister Beetle.'

'That doesn't make any sense. Why should the sign have been made by the Ocotillo Kid? What were you doin' anywhere near the Blister Beetle in the first place?'

'Let's just say I've come across the Ocotillo Kid before. He's well known to be ridin' the owlhoot trail all around these parts. Some even say he's hidin' out someplace close.' As he spoke he watched Taggart, trying to place his role in the set-up.

'Who are you?' Taggart said. Fogarty

141

saw no reason to lie, until he recalled his real purpose in coming to the Blister Beetle. If Arrowsmith was around, it might not be a good idea to give his actual name. 'The name's Henderson,' he said.

Taggart considered this for a few moments. 'Henderson,' he repeated. 'Seems like I ought to have heard that name before.'

Fogarty shrugged. 'There ain't anythin' unusual about it,' he replied.

Taggart appeared to be thinking about the situation. Fogarty was sure that he had hit on something, that he had touched a raw nerve. There was a connection between the Ocotillo Kid and the Blister Beetle, but how much did Taggart know about it? What would his attitude be? As far as his own fate was concerned, there was one obvious possibility, which would be for Taggart to let Robardes and his gang do what they had threatened to do. But Fogarty sensed that Taggart had been placed in an ambiguous position. Perhaps he was wondering if he, Fogarty, knew more than he was letting on, if maybe there were other people besides Fogarty who had suspicions about the Ocotillo Kid. If he was right, Fogarty thought it might not be a bad idea to play on Taggart's uncertainty, but without giving anything away.

'I'm a friend of Marshal Shackleton,' he said, 'back in Hackberry.'

Taggart's expression didn't change but Fogarty had a feeling that his confusion was increased. 'Trespassin' is a serious business,' he replied. 'I doubt whether he would approve.' He paused and then addressed Robardes over Fogarty's shoulder. 'Take him across to the bunkhouse,' he said, 'till I decide what to do with him.'

There was a stir of movement behind Fogarty, who got slowly to his feet. Robardes grabbed him by the arm and began to march him towards the door.

'No funny business,' Taggart said. 'Just keep an eye on him. For now.'

6

After his talk with Arrowsmith, Baxter spent the rest of an anxious night thinking about what Arrowsmith had said, but his resolve was only strengthened. If Arrowsmith was right, the silver mine could be the answer to all his problems. It was better than having to rely on the Ocotillo Kid, and if the Kid succeeded in robbing the Dry Fork bank, he would have the wherewithal to develop it.

The more he thought it over, the more it seemed to him that the quicker he acted on what Arrowsmith had told him, the better it would be. He had been enjoying the opportunity the Kid's absence had provided for a spot of relaxation, but there would be time enough in due course for all that. Right now his best interests would be served by taking action. He needed to check out the silver mine, and do it quickly.

For his part, Arrowsmith was resigned to cutting Baxter in on the silver mine. Unlike Fogarty, Baxter had the necessary influence. Having him along meant that the mine could be developed. He wasn't in a position to know anything about Baxter's real financial situation. As far he was concerned, Baxter was the man he needed.

As he and Baxter rode away from the Blister Beetle in the early morning, he was feeling fairly satisfied. Certainly things seemed better than they had been for some time. There was still one thing he needed to do, however, and that was to deal with Fogarty. Again, Baxter's support could prove more than useful. Baxter wouldn't be the type to let anyone stand in his way. Arrowsmith knew him of old. Yes, with Baxter along, he had little to fear from Fogarty. And after all, hadn't he successfully dealt with Henderson?

* * *

Marshal Shackleton waited patiently for the return of Fogarty, but as time passed he began to grow more anxious. He suddenly realized that he had no clear idea what Fogarty intended doing about Arrowsmith. He wondered whether Fogarty himself knew. Maybe it would have been more sensible to have simply ridden up to the Blister Beetle and announce what they had come for. He had the authority of his marshal's badge, after all.

Even as the thought occurred to him he realized that the badge probably meant nothing at all. Strictly speaking, he was outside the area of its jurisdiction. In any case, if his growing suspicions about Baxter were correct, the owner of the Blister Beetle wasn't likely to show it much respect.

The night seemed endless. Above him the constellations slowly wheeled. He smoked one cigarette after another but he couldn't dismiss the thoughts that occupied his brain. Was everything OK back in Hackberry? What about

Cora? What about Somersby? More immediately, what was happening with Fogarty? He got to his feet and began to prowl about. It seemed to him one moment that the sky was beginning to lighten, and then in the next the night seemed darker than ever. He listened to the sound of the horses' breathing and walked across to stroke them. What was Fogarty up to?

He couldn't wait any longer. He had to do something. He would just have to take his chance and do what he should have done in the first place: ride to the Blister Beetle, demand to know whether Arrowsmith was there, and if so, place him under arrest. If that meant he had to delay getting on the trail of the Ocotillo Kid, then that was the way it would have to be.

The only question was whether he should wait till morning. It made sense to do so. It would seem very odd to arrive at the ranch house in the middle of the night. But he was too worried about what might have happened to

Fogarty to delay. With a final glance about him, he climbed into leather and, leading the second horse, began to make for the Blister Beetle.

* * *

The Ocotillo Kid and his gang rode hard till they were well clear of the railroad. Eventually they drew rein and came to a halt. 'We done it, boys!' the Kid shouted. There was an outburst of shouting and cheering.

'Let's take a look at what we got,' somebody called. The uproar redoubled; some were in favour of opening the safe on the spot by whatever means it took, others, more cautious, were for getting back to the Blister Beetle. The Kid allowed his men to have their heads till at length he drew his six-gun and fired into the air. 'I got a better idea!' he shouted. There was silence while he paused so that his next words would have maximum effect.

'What I say is, let's celebrate!' he then

exclaimed. 'We ain't in any rush. We'll deal with the safe and then take a little detour and head for Hackberry. That's what we told Robardes, after all.'

It took a moment for his words to sink in, then the gunslicks began to whoop and halloo afresh. The Kid grinned. Everything they needed for a good time was waiting for them at his brother's saloon. There was liquor and there were women. He felt like celebrating.

'We're gonna have us the time of our lives,' he shouted. 'We're gonna tear that town apart. Hackberry ain't gonna know what hit it!'

* * *

Baxter and Arrowsmith, riding up into the hills and following the course of the stream, had passed the point at which Arrowsmith and Fogarty had panned for gold. They carried on along the crest of a ridge through thickets of scrub oak and acacia. Although they were quite high, the heat was oppressive. They followed the trail along the base of a cliff till it began to grow steeper, when Arrowsmith signalled for them to halt.

'This is about as far as we go on horseback,' he said.

They dismounted and after knee-haltering the horses, moved forward on foot. Baxter was finding the going tough, and not for the first time he questioned the wisdom of leaving the comforts of the Blister Beetle behind to embark on such an enterprise. They hadn't gone far, however, when Arrowsmith pointed ahead and Baxter saw what appeared to be the mouth of a cave. When they had scrambled and climbed the rest of the way, he saw it wasn't a cave but the entrance to a tunnel.

'Is this it?' Baxter snapped.

'I know it maybe don't look like much,' Arrowsmith replied, 'but believe me, there's a fortune in silver here just waitin' to be dug out.'

Baxter approached the tunnel entrance. It was low and narrow and when he bent down and peered inside he could not see very far because the light was soon swallowed up in blackness. His first impressions were not favourable.

'Look over here,' Arrowsmith said. Without waiting for a reply, he turned away and began to walk further down the trail. It took a slight curve and then he stopped. 'There!' he said with a hint of triumph in his voice. Baxter looked up at the cliff face. 'Can't you see? This is just one of the places where the ore comes to the surface.'

At first Baxter's untrained eye could detect nothing unusual, but as Arrowsmith continued to draw his attention to a small area of the cliff face, he saw what he took to be the outcrop.

'The lode runs west at this point,' Arrowsmith said. 'It dips down where the oldster started the tunnel.'

'Why didn't he sink his shaft here?' Baxter said.

151

'I don't know,' Arrowsmith replied. 'I guess he knew what he was doin', him or whoever he was with back then.'

Baxter was feeling a little more convinced as he and Arrowsmith walked back to the tunnel.

'Let's take a look, see how far it goes,' Arrowsmith said. He produced a candle and lit it.

'You go first,' Baxter said. Arrowsmith bent down and entered the tunnel. It was very narrow but it soon opened up and Baxter could see that the roof was now supported by timber props. He suddenly became conscious of being buried beneath a mountain.

'I reckon that's far enough,' he said.

Arrowsmith glanced over his shoulder. 'Are you sure? If we go a little further you'll see where a ladder leads up to another gallery. I figure they were well on the way to reachin' the ore.'

'I'm sure,' Baxter said. 'Let's turn round and go back.'

They made their way to the entrance.

As they emerged, the sunlight dazzled their eyes.

'What do you think, then?' Arrowsmith said. 'I figure with that shaft already started, it wouldn't take a lot to make the mine a goin' concern.'

Baxter thought for a few moments. 'What do you reckon it's gonna take?' he asked.

'I ain't no expert. I figured you might know more about it than me.'

'I know somethin',' Baxter replied. 'If we're gonna get beyond the surface veins, we'll need to dig deeper. That's gonna require steam engines to haul the ore and pump out water. We'll probably need to dig new shafts. They'll need to be supported.'

His eyes swept the terrain. 'There isn't a lot of timber,' he said. 'That's gonna be a problem. Then there's the whole question of transport.'

He was talking to himself as much as to Arrowsmith. It was going to take a huge investment. A small arastra would be no good for crushing the ore. A great vista began to open out to his imagination: crushing mills, rock-breakers, stamps, rails, machinery. It was a daunting prospect, but at the same time a stimulating one. Once again his thoughts turned to the Ocotillo Kid. If he came up trumps with the bank-robbery caper . . . He turned back to Arrowsmith. 'It's gonna need a lot of plannin',' he said.

'But you're interested, Mr Baxter?'

Baxter looked around him. In his mind's eye he conjured a vision of how it might look, of how it might be.

'I got to think about it,' he replied. 'Maybe there's somethin' in it.'

* * *

As Marshal Shackleton approached the Blister Beetle he was surprised to see that lights were showing both in the ranch house windows and in the bunkhouse. If Baxter was around it made his task easier. As he swung down from the saddle a group of men appeared from the shadows.

'Funny time to be payin' a courtesy call,' one of them said.

'It ain't a courtesy call. I'm here on business: law business.' He turned to show the man his badge. The man looked closely and an ugly grin spread across his features.

'Now ain't that a coincidence?' he said. 'You're the second person we caught snoopin' about.'

The marshal did not reply, but it occurred to him that the second person could only be Fogarty.

'Yeah,' the man continued. 'And here's another coincidence. The first *hombre* we caught claimed to be a friend of the marshal of Hackberry. Now, I wonder if that could be you?'

Shackleton was wondering how to play the situation when the issue was taken out of his hands as the ranch house door opened and another man appeared on the veranda. Shackleton could see that it wasn't Baxter.

'What's goin' on now, Robardes?' the man asked. 'Hell, I figured you

boys would have settled down by now.'
Before the man could say anything, the
marshal spoke.

'The name's Shackleton. I'm a
United States Marshal. I would like to
have words with Mr Baxter. Where is
he?'

'He ain't here. I'm lookin' after the
Blister Beetle while he's away on
business.'

'Perhaps I'd better explain what I'm
doin' here. I've been trackin' a man
called Arrowsmith and the trail leads
right here to the Blister Beetle.'

The man turned to Robardes. 'Get
back over to the bunkhouse,' he said.

Robardes exchanged glances with the
rest of the men and one of them
mumbled something beneath his breath
before they reluctantly moved away.
The other man watched them go before
turning back to Shackleton.

'Guess I'd better introduce myself,'
he said. 'I'm Taggart. I'm the foreman
of the Blister Beetle. I guess you might
as well come on in.'

Shackleton fastened his horse to the hitch rail and followed Taggart inside the ranch house. 'You sure seem to be keepin' late hours,' he said. Taggart motioned to a chair and the marshal sat down.

'It's been a strange night,' Taggart said. He looked closely at Shackleton. 'You say you're lookin' for a man named Arrowsmith? You've chosen to come at a mighty odd time. Might I ask what your business is with him?'

Shackleton returned Taggart's gaze. It seemed to him that Taggart looked anxious. He was tempted to mention Fogarty's name but until he had a better idea of the set-up on the Blister Beetle he decided for the moment to play his cards close to his chest. After all, Robardes had already unwittingly given him the information he required.

'Arrowsmith might also be using the name Packard. Either way, he's wanted on suspicion of murder, amongst other things,' he replied.

As he spoke he observed the other

man's expression closely. It seemed to him that the name meant something to him. There was a pause, which Shackleton wasn't going to be the first to break. Taggart's hand reached up to scratch his stubbled chin.

'There was a man here recently,' he said eventually. 'I don't know that he answered to either of those names, but maybe he's the one you're lookin' for.'

'Where is he now?'

'He left with Mr Baxter.'

'Did he say where?'

Taggart paused for a moment. 'He mentioned somethin' about the hills, but nothin' more than that.'

The marshal pondered his words before speaking again. 'Those two who greeted me just now,' he said. 'They didn't seem to be too friendly.'

'It's late,' Taggart replied. 'What did you expect?'

'I'd have expected them to be gettin' some shuteye,' the marshal replied. 'Seems like they keep mighty late hours.'

Taggart shrugged. 'That's Robardes and some of his *compadres*,' he replied.

'Kinda surplus to requirements, ain't they?'

'What do you mean?'

'From what I could see of the place as I rode in, there didn't seem to be much requirement for a lot of ranch hands.'

'Mr Baxter has plans. It ain't my job to ask questions.'

'Well, I might have one or two to ask them. You wouldn't mind if I take a stroll over to the bunkhouse?' Taggart looked uncomfortable. 'It ain't as if I'd be disturbin' anybody,' Shackleton added.

'They won't be able to tell you anythin' I can't,' Taggart said.

'Maybe not. But I'd like to ask them anyway.'

Taggart dithered for another moment before replying. 'OK. I'll take you over there myself. Just give me a moment.'

The marshal got to his feet while Taggart opened a drawer, took a six-gun from it and thrust it into his trouser belt. Neither man made any comment. There were things puzzling Shackleton, but his purpose was fixed. He had to find Fogarty. He was somewhere nearby but the marshal was pretty sure that he wasn't in the ranch house. He had to be careful how he played his hand, but he knew the game.

Taggart's mind, on the other hand, was a mass of confusion. Was Shackleton telling the truth? Henderson had mentioned his name. That was strange, but what was the link between them? Henderson had said he was on the trail of the Ocotillo Kid but the marshal had talked about someone else called Arrowsmith. Or Packard. Was Arrowsmith the man Baxter had ridden off with? If so, why?

Behind all the other questions racking his brain was the bigger question: what was the truth about Baxter's brother? There certainly seemed to be a lot more to the relationship than met the eye, else why were so many obvious gunslingers making free of the Blister Beetle? In view of what Henderson had said, it seemed he was right to be suspicious. And he had told Robardes to take charge of Henderson. Assuming he had carried out his orders, Henderson was at the bunkhouse right now.

He led the way through the door and onto the veranda. The air was chill and the stars blazed overhead with an icy fire. Light spilled from the door of the bunkhouse and the sound of voices carried on the breeze. Taggart looked sideways at Shackleton as they moved, but the marshal's eyes were fixed steadily ahead.

They came to the bunkhouse; the door stood slightly ajar and Taggart nudged it open. As he did so a shot rang out and he staggered backwards. Shackleton's gun was in his hand and as he grabbed Taggart, he opened fire. Somebody behind the door shrieked and then all hell seemed to break loose. The door sprang wide and a sheet of flame and lead poured through it. Stabs of flame appeared at the windows. Shackleton and Taggart stumbled backwards as bullets tore up the dirt all around them. The two men hit the ground and managed to crawl to the relative shelter of a water trough.

'Are you hit?' Shackleton yelled.

'Yes, but I don't think it's too bad.'

The marshal glanced sideways at Taggart. His left arm hung limply and blood oozed from his upper arm.

'What the hell is goin' on?' the marshal shouted.

'I don't know. Looks like Robardes and his boys are cuttin' up for some reason,' Taggart responded.

Shackleton did not reply. He had a sudden intuition what that reason might be, and as if to confirm it he suddenly heard a voice as it rose above the uproar.

'Shackleton! I'm up here!'

The voice seemed to come from the heavens; Shackleton looked up and saw the figure of Fogarty on the roof of the bunkhouse. Although their position was desperate, he felt a surge of relief. Bullets were whining and singing as they struck the metal of the water trough and it was imperative that he and Taggart find a better position. Fogarty seemed to realize it too.

'Hang on!' he shouted. 'I'll swing down and get in a position to cover you so you can make a break.'

'OK, but make it quick!' Shackleton replied.

Fogarty moved quickly to the edge of the bunkhouse roof furthest away from where Shackleton and Taggart crouched. He swung his legs over the edge, then dropped from sight. In a few moments he reappeared, running hard for an outbuilding from which he could get a good sight on the bunkhouse.

'Get ready to run,' Shackleton warned Taggart. Taggart nodded. His face was creased with pain and the marshal wondered if he understood the situation. There was no time for delay, however. He had run out of bullets and once Robardes and his boys realized it, their situation would be truly untenable.

He looked towards the outhouse. Fogarty raised his rifle and then, swinging it back round and taking a bead on the bunkhouse door, commenced firing.

'Now!' Shackleton yelled. He and Taggart got to their feet and, doubled over, began to run pell-mell for the ranch house. Behind them they could hear the sustained racket of Fogarty's rifle. What had happened to him? How had he acquired the weapon? Even as he ran Shackleton's brain was asking questions. Fogarty was doing a good job. Lead sang through the air close by but it was nothing like the concentrated fire they had endured behind the water tank. Struggling for breath, they rounded a corner of the ranch house and pulled up.

'What's goin' on?' Taggart panted, repeating Shackleton's earlier question.

'Your guess is as good as mine,' Shackleton replied. 'Right now we got to reload and get in a position to support Fogarty.'

'Fogarty?' Taggart said.

'Don't pretend you don't know him,' Shackleton replied. He looked at Taggart's pallid face. 'Are you sure you can manage?' he added.

Taggart grimaced but there was determination written across his features. 'I'll be all right,' he said.

Without waiting further, Shackleton led the way back inside the ranch house. There was a rack of rifles on the wall and they each grabbed one.

'There's ammo in the drawer,' Taggart hissed.

They loaded up, then ran through to a back room which gave them a view of the bunkhouse. Smashing the glass with their rifle butts, they prepared to open fire.

Shackleton glanced at Taggart. The man was clearly in a lot of pain but he was concentrating hard on the task in hand. He looked across at the outbuilding where Fogarty had taken up a position, but he did not have a clear view of that part of it and he couldn't see his friend. He turned his attention back to the bunkhouse, drawing a bead on the doorway. He became conscious of the ticking of a clock in the other room.

The moments slipped by and turned into minutes and suddenly he became aware that the sounds of shooting had stopped. It was strange that he had not noticed it before; as soon as he registered the fact the silence seemed to become palpable. He looked over at Taggart. The man was slumped against the wall. He seemed to have passed out and Shackleton hadn't noticed that either. Then the silence was rent by the sound of Fogarty's voice calling from out of the void.

'Shackleton, can you see anythin'?'

'Nope. I can't hear anythin' either!'

'Where are you?'

'We're inside the ranch house. I've got a good view of the bunkhouse but I can't see any signs of movement.'

There was a pause and Fogarty called out again. 'Don't move. I'm comin'!'

Shackleton ducked under the window and examined the still form of Taggart. The man had clearly fainted. It was obvious that he had lost a lot of blood and Shackleton, untying his neckerchief, did what he could to bind his wounded arm. By the time he had fastened a rough tourniquet, he could hear footsteps in the other room and Fogarty appeared.

'Hell, it's good to see you, Shackleton,' he said.

'Yeah, and you. But what the hell is happenin'?'

'Robardes and his crew caught me. They were holdin' me in the bunkhouse. There was some sort of disturbance and I took my chance.'

'That was probably when I turned up,' Shackleton said.

Fogarty glanced at the inert figure of Taggart. 'Is he . . . ?'

'He's wounded but he'll be OK. Anyway, we can save this conversation till we've found out what's become of Robardes.' They looked through the window frame at the bunkhouse.

'Seems mighty quiet,' Shackleton said.

'There was quite an outburst of fire when you made your break,' Fogarty said, 'but then it went quiet and there's been nothin' from Robardes since.'

They glanced outside once again. 'Guess there's only one way to find out,' Shackleton said, 'and that's to go and take a look.'

'Too big a risk,' Fogarty said. 'It could be some kind of a ruse.'

Shackleton shrugged. Fogarty grinned. 'I'll go back the same way I got here. Nobody'll see me. There's some bushes at the back for shelter. Wait here and keep me covered.'

'Like hell,' Shackleton said. 'Lead the way, I'm comin' with you.'

After checking once more that Taggart was OK for the time being, they went through the other room and out of the door. Fogarty led them round the opposite side to the outbuilding. They moved round it. As Fogarty had said, there was cover at the rear of the bunkhouse and they quickly reached it. Once they had done so, what had happened was immediately apparent. There was a back entrance to the bunkhouse leading into the bushes, which had been trampled and pushed aside.

'Looks like they decided to make a getaway, but why?' Fogarty said.

Cautiously, they pushed through the undergrowth. At a little distance they found a corral still containing a couple of horses and the unmistakable indications that a group of horsemen had only recently ridden away.

'No doubt about it. They've gone,' Fogarty said.

Shackleton shook his head. 'I don't get it. Maybe we'll find some answers back at the bunkhouse.'

They made their way through the undergrowth and approached the bunkhouse with care. The back entrance stood open. They positioned themselves on either side of the doorframe and then, at a signal from Shackleton, threw themselves inside.

The place was empty apart from three bodies which lay on the floor near the front. Shackleton inspected them. Two were dead but the third was only wounded in the thigh. He looked up at the marshal through pain-clouded eyes. Shackleton inspected the wound and did what he could to stanch the bleeding. As he finished Fogarty came up with a bottle of whiskey in his hand.

'There's more where that came from,' he said to Shackleton, and to the injured man: 'Here, take a drink.'

When the man had done so he seemed to be a lot better. He managed to hoist himself into a sitting position with his back against a bunk.

'OK,' Shackleton said. 'Start talkin'.'

The man looked blank.

'Why did Robardes open fire on Taggart? Where have the rest of 'em gone?'

The man still seemed reluctant to speak.

'In case you ain't noticed, I'm a United States Marshal. We've already got enough on you to put you behind bars for a long time. You might just stand a chance of a more lenient sentence if you're prepared to talk.'

Fogarty offered the man the bottle and he took a few more long swigs of the whiskey. Between them, the liquor and the marshal's words seemed to have an effect.

'Robardes has gone to join up with Goffin,' he said.

'You mean, the Ocotillo Kid?' Fogarty replied.

The man looked up at him through bleary eyes. 'Yes,' he said. 'That's what folks call him.'

'So what's the Ocotillo Kid got to do with the Blister Beetle?'

The man hesitated for a moment and the marshal seized him by the collar. 'I'm losin' patience,' he snapped. The man winced.

'OK, OK,' he replied. 'I ain't exactly sure, but I think the Ocotillo Kid is Baxter's brother.'

Shackleton and Fogarty exchanged glances. 'So the Kid uses this place as a hideout?' Shackleton said. 'Hell, it's beginnin' to make sense.' He released his hold and the man's head sank back against the bunk. 'Robardes is one of the Ocotillo Kid's gang. Then where is the Kid?'

'I don't know,' the man replied. Shackleton's response was to seize hold of him again. 'I don't know where he's been, but he said, if he weren't back by tonight to meet up with him in town.'

'In town?'

'In Hackberry. I guess that's where Robardes has gone.'

'And our arrival threatened to upset his plans. What's Taggart's role in all this?'

'Taggart don't know nothin' about it. He ain't one of the gang.'

Shackleton turned to Fogarty. 'I clean forgot about Taggart till now,' he

said. 'I guess we'd better get back to th
ranch house and see how he is.'

'What you gonna do with me?' the
man said.

Shackleton considered the question.
'I ought to take you in,' he said, 'but I
got other things to worry about right
now. Do you figure you could ride a
horse?'

'Sure. If someone can help me onto
it.'

Shackleton looked up at Fogarty.
'Give me a hand to lift him,' he said.
'We'll take him to the corral and put
him on one of those horses. After that
it's down to him.'

When they had carried out the plan
and returned to the ranch house, they
were surprised to see Taggart sitting up
and looking a lot better.

'Did you know the Ocotillo Kid is
Baxter's brother?' Shackleton asked him.

Taggart shook his head. 'I figured
somethin' was goin' on and I could
have made a few guesses, but I didn't
know for sure.'

'This man who rode off with Baxter. What did you say his name was?'

Taggart thought for a moment. 'I don't know,' he concluded. 'He didn't mention it to me.'

'What did he look like?'

'Kinda nondescript,' Taggart said.

'That ain't much help,' Shackleton commented.

'Did you see what kind of a horse he was ridin'?' Fogarty asked.

'Yeah. It was a grulla.'

Fogarty snapped his fingers in his excitement. 'Arrowsmith rode a grulla. It's gotta be him.'

'When will they be back?' Shackleton rapped.

'Baxter didn't say. But he did mention somethin' about spendin' time at the Hungry Loop if things turned out like he hoped.'

'The Hungry Loop? That's the saloon he owns in Hackberry,' the marshal said to Fogarty. He thought for a moment. 'I figure we need to get back to Hackberry,' he said, 'and pretty quick.'

Fogarty nodded in agreement. 'Seem like the Kid is headin' that way,' he said. 'If Baxter turns up there too, so much the better. If not, I'll catch up with him later and find out where I can catch up with Arrowsmith.'

'You need a doc,' Shackleton said to Taggart. 'You can ride to town with us.'

'Sure thing,' Taggart replied, 'but I ain't comin' just to go to the doc's. I got a score to settle with the Ocotillo Kid too. Not to mention Robardes. I might have taken a hit, but I ain't out of the game. If it comes to a showdown with the Ocotillo Kid, count me in.'

Shackleton's stern features relaxed a little. 'I guess you ain't, at that,' he said. 'OK, let's get ready to ride.'

7

Deputy Marshal Somersby and Cora sat in the local eating house having lunch together. Cora's face was flushed, but it wasn't just because she had been riding.

'You seem pleased with yourself,' Somersby remarked.

'I've been talkin' to Miss Mather.'

'The schoolma'am?'

'Yes, and she thinks she can offer me some work teaching. It would only be part-time at first, but it might lead on to something more.'

'That's fine,' Somersby said. 'I reckon the town's on the up. Once the railroad extends this far there'll be plenty of folk wantin' to move in. The school will need to expand.' He paused. 'Does that mean you're committed to stayin' in Hackberry?'

She gave him an upward glance. 'I

came a long way to be with Uncl Clem,' she said. 'It would be silly to return. Anyway, there's nothing for me now back East and I like it here.'

Somersby shuffled uncomfortably. 'Say,' he said, 'can I pour you another coffee?'

As he leaned forward to do so, the door burst open and an elderly man came in. He looked quickly round and, seeing Somersby, came rushing over to him. 'Somebody said you were in here,' he said.

Somersby looked up at him. 'What is it, Hornsby?' he said.

'I think you'd better get on over to the Hungry Loop,' the oldster replied. 'There's some mean *hombres* in there and I think there's gonna be trouble.'

Cora looked anxiously at Somersby as he replaced the coffee pot and got to his feet. He walked to the door, opened it and glanced down the street. A number of horses were tied to the hitch rail outside the Hungry Loop. Sounds of shouting and raucous laughter eached his ears.

He turned back to Hornsby. 'Just give me a minute,' he said. 'I'll be right over.'

The oldster nodded and went back through the open door. Somersby walked across to the counter and paid for the meal. Cora got up from the table and joined him. 'Come back with me,' she said.

'I'll be over just as quick as I can,' he replied.

They came out of the café and he walked with her to the junction on the way to Shackleton's house. Even at that distance the noise from the Hungry Loop reached their ears.

'You carry on,' he said.

She clutched at his arm. 'Please be careful,' she breathed.

He looked down at her, then suddenly his arms were round her. He breathed the fragrance of her hair and then put his hand beneath her chin and tipped up her face. He was surprised to see that her eyes were moist. Without thinking he pressed his lips to hers. She responded and they kissed several times before eventually drawing back.

'I'm sorry,' he mumbled. 'I didn't mean to take advantage.'

'Don't be silly,' she said. 'I've been hoping you would do that since we first started riding together.'

He was about to respond when a shot rang out from the direction of the saloon. 'I've got to go,' he said. 'Hurry straight back. I'll see you soon.'

She looked pleadingly at him. 'Please be careful,' she repeated. She turned and walked quickly away. For a moment he watched her, then, adjusting his gunbelt, he set off in the direction of the Hungry Loop.

*   *   *

Shackleton, Fogarty and Taggart rode hard away from the Blister Beetle. The words of the injured gunslinger had got Shackleton worrying about Somersby, and he was beginning to feel guilty bout having left him in charge of things at Hackberry.

The quicker they got back to town, the better it would be. Even though they made good time Robardes and his gang remained ahead of them. It was easy, however, to follow their sign.

'If I didn't know better, I'd say they knew we were on their trail,' Shackleton suggested.

'Once Fogarty got loose they sure didn't fancy stayin' to make a fight of it,' Taggart said.

'If our friend back at the bunkhouse is correct, Robardes is plannin' to rendezvous with the Ocotillo Kid. He probably figures there's safety in numbers.'

Shackleton cast a steely eye on his companions. 'He's probably right,' he went on. 'I don't how many gunslicks the Kid's got at his command, but we're clearly gonna be outnumbered.'

'There's plenty of 'em,' Taggart said. 'The only good thing is that they seem to be well spread out. The Ocotillo Kid covers a lot of territory.'

'My old friend Ahiga would testify to that,' Fogarty said.

'I don't figure they'd stick around for long with the Kid out of the way.'

'I hope you're right,' Fogarty answered.

'Well, with any luck we're about to find out,' the marshal concluded.

They looked at one another grimly before riding on. 'I guess we are, at that,' Fogarty agreed.

★ ★ ★

As Deputy Marshal Somersby walked towards the Hungry Loop saloon, he became conscious that the street was deserted. Yet it had been quite an active scene not long before, when he had been sitting in the café with Cora. He became aware, too, of a hollow feeling in the pit of his stomach and dryness in his throat. He swallowed hard and licked his lips. The noise emanating from the saloon grew louder. Yelling and shouting were interspersed with wild whoops and howls and then, once again, the loud report of a gun.

The deputy stepped up to the board-walk and pushed aside the batwing doors. The atmosphere of the saloon was fetid with smoke and the smell of liquor. People were sitting at the tables playing cards but the largest number were gathered at the bar around a man with a smoking gun in his hand. A shattered mirror told the tale of what had just happened. Somersby felt like an automaton that someone had wound up as he approached the group. The noise abated slightly and a few of the men seemed to notice him for the first time. He carried on walking till he faced the man with the revolver.

'OK,' he said, 'you've had your fun. Now give me the gun.'

The man looked at him with a look of surprise on his face, which soon gave way to an ugly leer. 'Who are you?' he said.

'I'm the law and the law says no weapons allowed. Better check it in.'

The man turned to his drunken

companions. 'Hell,' he said, 'didn[
anybody see a notice? Now you done
got me in trouble with the marshal
here.' His words were greeted by hoots
of laughter. 'Better do as the man says,
Robardes!' someone shouted. 'He's
scarin' me!'

With a smirk on his face, Robardes
made to hand the gun over to
Somersby. As the deputy marshal
stepped forward to take it, Robardes
suddenly swung the gun so that it
pointed at Somersby's chest. 'Now
make me check it in,' he said.

Somersby glanced about him. The
gang of men had spread out so that he
was surrounded. The general hubbub
had ceased and the people seated at the
tables had stopped their activities to
stare expectantly at what was happening. A few were surreptitiously trying to
edge away from the action. Somersby
turned his attention back to the man
addressed as Robardes. The man's eyes
seemed to bore into his own.

'Don't do anything foolish. Just hand

over,' Somersby managed to say.

There was no response from Robardes. His features were cold and distant as his finger tightened on the trigger of the gun.

Even as he did so, the pregnant silence was riven by a shattering roar and Robardes reeled backwards, clutching at his shoulder and dropping his weapon. Instinctively Somersby's hand dropped to his holster and as his gun sprang into his hand the scene erupted into a tumult of flame and smoke.

Somersby swivelled and opened fire. Another gunman staggered backwards and the deputy felt a bullet whistle past his face as he dived for cover. Bullets thudded into the floor and a chandelier burst upon the ground in a shower of glass.

Then, quite suddenly, the uproar ceased and stillness descended like a heavy weight. As the smoke cleared Somersby could see that only one of the gunmen was left standing with his arms in the air. Footsteps sounded through the silence and

turning his head in the directio[n]
which they came, Somersby saw a [man]
advancing towards him. He gripped his g[un]
thinking it must be another of Robarde[s]
men, when he recognized the familiar
figure of Ahiga.

'Somersby,' the Navajo said, 'are you
OK?'

The deputy marshal's head was
ringing with the noise and he felt
disorientated, but Ahiga's words had
the effect of a cold douche. 'I think so,'
he replied.

'You did good,' Ahiga said.

Somersby got to his feet. 'I'd be a
dead man if you hadn't got here when
you did.'

Ahiga advanced to where the inert
form of Robardes lay slumped by the
bar and bent down. 'He's alive,' he said.
He stood up again and after examining
the other three, shook his head.
Robardes began to moan and made a
move to sit up. Ahiga looked from him
to the man still standing with his arms
held up.

,' he said to Somersby, 'I guess, you're the law, you'd better put those two in the jailhouse.'

By the time Somersby had carried out his duties with regard to the two prisoners, the sun was low in the sky. The doctor had removed a bullet from Robardes's shoulder and as Somersby left the marshal's office, slamming the door behind him, the last thing he heard were that gentleman's moans of pain and discontent. He quickly made his way towards the marshal's house; as he approached he was pleased to see Cora coming to meet him.

'Ahiga told me what happened,' she said.

He didn't want to worry her so he attempted to play down the whole affair. 'It was nothin' much,' he replied. 'Just a few people gettin' drunk and carryin' things too far.'

Suddenly she came close and leaned her head against his shoulder. He was taken aback and it took him a few moments to realize that she was shaking.

'Hey now, what's this all abo⟨⟩ said. He put his arms around he⟨⟩ held her close; she didn't reply but a⟨⟩ a few moments seemed to gath⟨⟩ herself together and stepped away. Her eyes were glistening.

'Anyway,' she resumed, 'I came to meet you because some other people have just arrived at the house.' He looked puzzled. 'My uncle and Mr Fogarty, to be exact.' She laughed. 'And they've got another friend with them, a Mr Taggart.'

A feeling of relief suddenly flooded through Somersby. Taking Cora by the hand, he quickened his step. 'What's been happenin' with them?' he asked.

'I don't know. They only just got here. In fact, they're putting up their horses in the stable right now. It's lucky I already put some supper on the stove.'

It was getting on for midnight by the time they had all eaten and told their respective stories. Cora had retired for the night, leaving the men to enjoy a

whiskey and cigars on the
—da.

…t's sure good to see you back in
…tion,' Fogarty said to Ahiga, 'although
i'm kinda surprised you're back on
your feet so quick.'

'Miss Siddons did a good job helpin''
to take care of me,' Ahiga replied.

'It's as well she did,' Somersby said.
'You sure cut it fine when you turned
up at the Hungry Loop.'

'That was against Miss Siddons's
orders. I was takin' a constitutional,'
Ahiga replied. 'I heard the noise
comin' from the saloon and then saw
you go in. I figured you might need
some help.'

Silence descended while they drank
and smoked. They were all thinking the
same thing, but it was the marshal who
eventually broached the subject.

'It seems like the Ocotillo Kid is on
his way,' he said. 'In fact, he could be
here any time. We got to do somethin''
about it.'

'Thanks to Somersby and Ahiga, we

already dealt with some of the varmints,' Fogarty said.

'It seems like the Kid was due to meet up with Robardes. The fact that he turned up here in Hackberry only confirms it,' Taggart added.

Ahiga got up to stretch his leg. 'Are you sure you can get around?' Fogarty asked.

Ahiga grinned. 'It's a bit stiff,' he said, 'but nothin's gonna keep me out of this.'

Shackleton took a long drag on his cigar. 'OK,' he said. 'If Ahiga's up to it, that makes the five of us. The Kid's gonna have a lot more at his disposal.'

'Five is fine,' Fogarty interjected.

The marshal grinned. 'Yeah, I figure you're right. Especially if we do somethin' to tip the odds just a little more in our favour.'

'What do you mean?' Somersby asked.

'What I mean is this. We either wait for the Kid to arrive in town, or we go out to meet him.'

'We don't know what direction he'll be comin' from,' Taggart said.

'Oh yes we do,' the marshal replied. 'Fogarty and I saw his sign when we were ridin' to the Blister Beetle. He was headed towards Dry Fork. So it's fair to assume he'll be comin' in on the trail from Dry Fork.'

'We don't know when he'll get here,' Somersby said.

'No, but it can't be long. In fact, it might be just long enough for us to take up position and intercept him.'

Fogarty was thoughtful. 'You know the territory better than any of the rest of us,' he said. 'Have you got someplace in mind?'

'Yes. Organ Pipe Gap. It's a narrow gorge. I figure we could give the Ocotillo Kid a real surprise.'

Somersby slapped his knee. 'Yes, of course,' he said. 'And it ain't far from town. It's the ideal spot.'

The others looked at each other. 'Sounds like a good plan to me,' Fogarty said. The marshal waited a few moments before taking the bottle and topping up their glasses.

'Let's take a drink to stoppin' the Ocotillo Kid in his tracks,' he said. As Fogarty threw back his drink, he was adding the name of Ben Arrowsmith.

*　*　*

At that very moment the man in question was sitting in his room at the Hungry Loop. He was still tired and saddle-sore following his trip back from the hills with Baxter, but his seething brain wouldn't allow him the option of sleep. He needed Baxter, but he didn't trust him. He seemed to have convinced Baxter about the feasibility of developing the mine, but he had an uncomfortable feeling that maybe he hadn't played his hand correctly.

Perhaps he should have concealed the exact whereabouts of the mine. That way, Baxter would have had to rely on him. As it was, Baxter might get to thinking that he was now surplus to requirements. After all, a fortune shared was a fortune halved. Furthermore, it was Baxter who would be supplying most of the finance. Arrowsmith had a feeling he was out of his depth, the same way he had felt when he had failed to deal with Fogarty.

That was something else he needed to think about. Was there some way he could get rid of Fogarty? Before he could do that, he needed to know where Fogarty was. He had been worried about the possibility of Fogarty being on his trail following the shooting of the Navajo. That, too, might have been a mistake. It would probably give Fogarty more reason to get even. The tangled thoughts went round in his head till he eventually fell into a troubled doze.

When he awoke day had dawned. He got to his feet, stumbled out onto the balcony of his room and looked down on the street. The town had not yet come to life but as he watched he suddenly shrank back into the shadows.

A group of horsemen had appeared. That was strange enough at this early hour, but as they passed beneath him he was certain that he recognized among them the man he had spent most of the night worrying about. It was Fogarty! And with him was the marshal. At the same moment a rapping at his door startled him. He moved back into the room and, drawing his six-gun, called through the door: 'Who is it?'

'Open up,' a voice hissed.

'Is that you, Mr Baxter?'

'Of course it is. Open the door.'

Arrowsmith became aware that he was shaking. When he opened the door, Baxter came in and gave him a curious look.

'Somethin' wrong, Arrowsmith?' he said. Without waiting for a reply he seized Arrowsmith by the shoulder. 'Did you see the marshal go ridin' by?'

Arrowsmith nodded his head.

'I got an idea it might be to our

advantage to follow him,' Baxter continued. 'Don't ask any questions. I'll explain as we go. Just take it from me we need to get on their trail. And I mean right now.'

★   ★   ★

Organ Pipe Gap lay sweltering in the late morning sun. The air danced and shimmered and even the huge saguaros looked shrivelled. Insects droned and buzzed and birds fluttered in the paloverde trees. Shackleton and his four companions had taken up positions near the entrance to the gap, and on the hillside above them Ahiga watched for any sign of the outlaws.

'Are you sure about this?' Taggart said to the marshal.

'I represent the law,' Shackleton replied. 'We ain't a gang of bushwhackers. I've got to give the Kid a chance to hand himself in.'

'You really think he's gonna do that?' Fogarty asked.

Somersby licked his lips. 'The marshal's right,' he said. 'We gotta do it like this.'

'What if they don't come this way?' Taggart said.

'They will if they're comin' from the direction of Dry Creek,' the marshal replied. They lapsed into silence, each thinking his own thoughts as the sun continued to climb. Suddenly they were roused by a call from Ahiga.

'Get ready! They're comin'!'

The Navajo scrambled back down the hillside to join them. They searched the terrain with their eyes but could see nothing.

'I hear their horses,' Ahiga said. Time passed and the marshal was beginning to think that Ahiga must have been mistaken when he detected a little smear of dust in the distance.

'Yup,' he muttered. 'We weren't wrong. Here they come.'

The cloud of dust grew bigger, travelling across the arid landscape like a whirlwind. As the riders drew closer, hrough the swirling clouds of dust they could see that there were at least fifteen of them, coming on at a steady trot. In the lead was a tall, spindly individual, who could only be the Ocotillo Kid.

The marshal stepped forward so that he was slightly ahead of the others, who began to string out across the entrance to the gap. As he made his move the group of riders drew to a halt. For a few moments they hesitated, then they came on again, moving slowly and reaching for their guns.

When he was within a few yards of Shackleton, the Kid stopped. He looked steadily at the marshal before glancing at the others.

'What is this?' he said.

'The game's up, Kid,' Shackleton replied.

The Kid pretended to be puzzled. 'I don't know what you mean, Marshal,' he said. He raised himself in the stirrups and looked back at his men. Some of them were grinning but others were looking tense. 'Hey boys, you got

any idea what the marshal's on ab[out]
He turned back to Shackleton. 'Me a[nd]
the boys have been workin' hard. W[e]
just want to ease down and spend a bit
of time relaxin' in town. Ain't no harm
in that now, is there?'

Shackleton reached into his pocket
and produced the worn Wanted poster
of the Ocotillo Kid. He held it out.

'Like I say, the game's up. I got more
men on the hillside. I suggest you save
yourselves a lot of trouble and hand
over your guns.'

The Ocotillo Kid stroked his chin in
an attitude of bravado but Fogarty
noticed his eyes flicker as he glanced up
at the slopes. 'You're makin' a big
mistake, Marshal,' he said.

The words were scarcely out of his
mouth when the tension was cut by the
loud report of a rifle from somewhere
on the hillside. It seemed almost to be a
confirmation of what the marshal had
said. Involuntarily, both groups of men
looked up towards where the shot had
come from, except for Fogarty and

a, whose eyes didn't leave the
laws, a few of whom had raised their
uns.

'Take cover!' Fogarty shouted. At the
same moment a rifle barked and a bullet
flew past his shoulder. He squeezed the
trigger of his Henry rifle and the outlaw
who had taken the shot fell from his
horse. There was further shooting from
the hillside and then the whole scene
disintegrated into a mêlée of panic and
confusion. Horses reared. Some of the
outlaws turned and began to ride away
while others began a fusillade of fire
aimed partly at Shackleton and his posse
and partly at the hillside.

Shackleton wasn't where he had
been. Together with the others, he had
taken cover behind the rocks and
boulders which stood at the entrance to
the gap. Glancing to his right, he saw
Somersby clutching one arm.

'Are you OK?' he shouted above the
din.

Somersby nodded and shouted something back but it was lost in an increased

198

cacophony of searing sound. Bull. whining among the rocks and sha. granite flew into the air. Fogarty's . was empty and he quickly jacked sor. more cartridges into the breech. Taking aim, he fired into the scrimmage of men and horses in front of him. The gunnies had either taken cover or ridden off. He looked for the Ocotillo Kid but couldn't see him. Then a bullet pinged off the rock uncomfortably close by. It had come from his rear and he turned over in order to take a look up at the hillside.

Someone was up there, the person who had fired the first shot. Who could it be? Had some of the gunslicks gone round a different way? Fogarty immediately rejected that option. They had seen the Ocotillo Kid and his gang from afar; there was no way they could have missed something like that. It had to be someone else, but who? And why had they opened fire? At first he had thought that whoever it was might have been aiming at the gunnies, but as more lead began to rain down on him from

...side, he realized that he was ...tely the target. Something needed ...be done. If he could get up the ...lside undetected, he might be able to put a stop to it. A higher spot would perhaps also give him a better position from which to fire down on the Kid and his gang.

He began to look about for a possible way up the hillside but there was nowhere that wasn't exposed. He looked back along the line of the gap; to his surprise he saw a figure just emerging from a patch of brush. As he watched another shot rang out from the hillside. It seemed there were two of them and one of them was apparently trying to get into a position behind Shackleton. Crawling to a point at which he felt it would be safe to stand upright, Fogarty began to work his way along the floor of the ravine. It was a risky thing to do, but there was just sufficient cover for him to avoid being hit by a bullet from whoever was still on the hillside.

The sounds of battle rang behind him. As he moved forward, kept his eyes fixed on the way ahead, expecting to come face to face with the stranger at some point. He hadn't seen anything of him since that first glimpse, till he suddenly spotted him again. He couldn't be sure, but whoever it was seemed to be moving in the same direction.

Then he realized that the man was not trying to get into a better position to fire on Shackleton, but was making a getaway. If so, the man on the hillside seemed uninterested. Maybe he too was under the impression that the stranger was trying to take up a better position. The man wasn't moving very quickly and Fogarty was catching up on him.

Presently he had a clearer view of him. Something about the man arrested his attention. Although it was only a back view, it looked familiar. Where had he seen that blue shirt and black leather waistcoat? Suddenly he realized with a shock who it was. It was the man he en looking for: Arrowsmith.

slight bend in the trail had carried
n him and his quarry out of sight of
ne mouth of the gap where the fighting
was taking place but Fogarty couldn't
be sure about the man on the hillside.
He was fast catching up with Arrowsmith, who hadn't yet noticed that
someone was coming up on him.
Arrowsmith was nearing the far end of
the gap. The time had come to act.
Stepping out into the pathway, Fogarty
called out: 'Arrowsmith! Turn right
around!'

Arrowsmith continued moving for a
few steps before stopping. He seemed
to consider the situation for a moment.
There was a brief pause and then
suddenly he spun round, the six-gun in
his hand spurting flame and lead. Two
bullets smashed into the hillside near
where Fogarty stood but he didn't
flinch. Arrowsmith squeezed the trigger
of his gun once more but it had either
run out of bullets or jammed. With a
curse he flung it from him and only

then did he look up to see who
he had been firing at.

'Fogarty!' he exclaimed.

Fogarty began to move forward,
taking one slow deliberate step after
another. His guns were still in their
holsters.

'Yeah, it's me, Fogarty. Finding you
here sure saves me a whole heap of
bother tryin' to hunt you down.'

Arrowsmith began to stumble backwards. 'I don't imagine what you think,
but you got things all wrong,' he said.

'I might have believed you if I didn't
have Ahiga for a witness.'

'Ahiga? Who the hell is Ahiga?'

'The man you ambushed and shot
after you saw me and him together.'

'That wasn't me. That was Henderson.'

Fogarty grinned. 'Just tell me one
thing,' he said. 'Why did you frame me
with the marshal back in Hackberry?'

Arrowsmith stumbled again. He
glanced quickly behind him, calculating
his chances if he took to his heels.

sn't like it seems,' he gasped. 'I
.' Sweat was dripping from his
w as he sought desperately to think
something that might fend off
Fogarty. 'Listen,' he said. 'I know where
there's a silver mine. I wanted to cut
you in on it all the time. I'm not lyin'. I
could take you there now. You could see
for yourself.'

Fogarty looked closely at him. 'Who's
that up on the hillside?' he asked.

'That's Baxter. He owns a ranch
called the Blister Beetle. The Ocotillo
Kid is his brother. It was him dragged
me along here. He figured you were
goin' after the Kid. He figured we
should warn him.'

'Why would he do that?'

'I don't know. Really, I don't know. I
think the Kid owes him some money.
Maybe just because he's his brother.'
Arrowsmith was panting with either
exertion or fear. He glanced desperately
behind him once more.

'That'll do,' Fogarty said. 'Wait right
there.' He reached down to his holster

and drew out one of his six-guns.

'What are you gonna do?' Arrowsmith said. 'Please, don't shoot!'

Fogarty weighed the gun in his hand and then threw it towards Arrowsmith. 'I'm giving you a chance,' he said, 'which is more than you just did for me. Pick up the gun and put it in your holster. Let's make this an equal fight.'

Arrowsmith hesitated.

'Go on,' Fogarty snapped. 'Pick it up and put it in your holster.'

Arrowsmith saw that it was no good trying to refuse. Stepping forward, he reached down and picked up the gun. In an instant he had pointed it at Fogarty and pulled the trigger. Quick as he was, Fogarty was quicker. As Arrowsmith's gun exploded, Fogarty's bullet caught him in the chest. He staggered back as the slug meant for Fogarty thudded harmlessly into the ground. Looking up, he gave Fogarty a look in which surprise and bewilderment were mingled, before crumpling to the ground. Fogarty moved to his side and kneeled beside him. A glance was enough to tell him that Arrowsmith was dead.

* * *

Marshal Shackleton had seen Fogarty move away, but he had no time to think about what he might be doing. The battle was raging around him. He could also see Somersby and Taggart, but there was no sign of Ahiga. There was no sign, either, of the Ocotillo Kid. It seemed to him, however, that the outlaws were in a better situation. The opening shot from the hillside seemed at first to have unsettled the gunnies, but they had the advantage of numbers and appeared to have settled for a battle of attrition. He was wondering what he might do to change that situation when suddenly all his calculations were terminated by a tremendous explosion which lifted him from his feet and threw him through the air. He landed with a heavy thud amid a cascade of rocks and debris. His head ached and he felt totally disorientated till he saw the figure of Somersby lying next to him. The deputy marshal's face was cut and bleeding but his eyes were open and he appeared to be OK. This was confirmed when Somersby opened his mouth and spoke.

'What was that?' he said.

'I don't know. But it sure in hell wasn't any kind of rifle shot.'

A dense cloud of smoke was billowing up from the entrance to the gap, obscuring the view of what lay beyond. Shackleton struggled to his feet, then helped up the younger man. Somersby winced as he did so.

'It's OK,' he said. 'A bullet burned my arm.' For a moment they stood in silence, gathering their wits, till Somersby spoke again.

'Nobody's shootin' any more,' he said.

It was true. The sounds of battle had vanished and as Shackleton and Somersby staggered through the haze of smoke and dust, the marshal began to think he might know the reason why. Lying in the path ahead they could see a body; when they got close they could see that it was Taggart. The marshal bent down to look at him. He was breathing. Shackleton straightened up and he and Somersby moved forward more carefully, anticipating a resumption of gunfire, but it didn't come. As they emerged into the open it was soon clear why. All around them lay the mangled bodies of the gunslicks. A few moans indicated that some of them were still alive.

'What happened?' Somersby said.

'Dynamite,' the marshal answered. 'The Kid and his gang must have been carrying dynamite and it's gone off. They were probably intendin' to throw it our way.'

'What? You figure it went off accidentally?'

'That's the way I see it. Can you think of a better explanation?'

They continued searching through

the scene of devastation till they were satisfied that they had accounted for all the outlaws in the vicinity. No doubt some of them had escaped either before or during the battle but the marshal wasn't concerned about them posing any threat. He was wondering what had become of Fogarty and Ahiga. He was also wondering what had become of the Ocotillo Kid since they had not found any corpse answering to his description.

*   *   *

After witnessing the demise of Arrowsmith, it seemed to Baxter that the time had come to make his getaway. His intervention on behalf of his brother had proved to be ineffectual. The Ocotillo Kid would have to take his chances. Taking care to keep under cover, he scrambled to the top of the slope and down the other side. As he approached the horses that he and Arrowsmith had left knee-haltered he heard the shattering noise of the explosion. He looked back, trying to work out what had happened. He didn't arrive at any conclusion except that it behoved him more than ever to get clear away from the whole scene. He stepped forward purposefully and had almost reached the horses when a man emerged from the bushes behind them.

'Hello, brother,' he said.

Baxter gasped. He hadn't expected to see the Ocotillo Kid. He observed now a third horse standing at a little distance. Its saddlebags were bulging. The Kid seemed to notice that Baxter's eyes were fixed on it.

'That's the loot,' he said. 'In fact, me and the boys were just on our way to town to blow some of it. We sure didn't expect this.'

Baxter's eyes were bright with greed. 'Whatever's goin' on down there,' he said, with a nod in the direction of the explosion, 'it don't do us any harm. We got the money. So much the better if there's no one else to share it with.'

An ugly leer spread across the Kid's

face. 'You sure got a point there,' he said.

Baxter looked at him questioningly. There was something in the tone of the Kid's voice that chilled him. 'Come on,' he said. 'What are we waitin' for? We got the money. Let's get out of here.'

The Kid gave an ugly laugh and the next moment Baxter was looking down the barrel of his gun. 'You ain't goin' nowhere,' the Kid said.

'What do you mean? We're wastin' time arguin' like this.' He made a move towards the horses but was stopped in his tracks by the sound of the Kid's gun being cocked.

'You don't expect me to believe you're here to try and help?' the Kid said. 'I ain't stupid. It was you set the marshal and his posse on to me.'

'Why would I do that?'

'You and me, we think alike, brother. You did it so you could have all the loot for yourself. Things were gettin' a little hot for you. You figured this would be the ideal way to get me off your back as well.'

'You're wrong. I never figured it that way. Hell, I didn't even know for sure you'd robbed the bank.'

'Not a bank,' the Kid said. 'A railroad train.'

'Whatever it was, it don't make any difference.'

'That's the way it's always been,' the Kid said. 'You let me take the risks and you take the rewards. Well, the situation's different now. I got the money and I don't intend sharin' it with no one. I guess the time's come for you to say your prayers.'

Baxter's hand moved upwards and he stroked his chin. The next moment it had dropped to the inside pocket of his jacket where he had a derringer concealed. The Kid suddenly realized what was happening and as Baxter drew the pistol his gun roared. Baxter staggered back and the Kid's gun belched flame once more. Baxter felt the hot lead tear into his chest; he had a

moment of agonizing pain and then he
didn't feel anything any more.

The Kid stood for a moment before
placing the gun back in its holster.
Then, without bothering further about
Baxter, he made for his horse and
sprang into the saddle. For a few
moments he sat there, feeling pretty
pleased with himself. A smile involuntarily broke out across his face. Things
had turned out OK. He had emerged
once and for all from under the shadow
of his brother and proved he wasn't a
man to be messed with. He had the
money. Once he had enjoyed it, it
wouldn't take him long to form a new
gang. Yes, he had come out of it pretty
well. He was just about to dig his spurs
into the horse's flanks when a voice
stopped him in his tracks.

'Hold it right there! One move and
you're dead!'

The Kid looked towards the sound of
the voice. Standing on a rock overlook-
ing the trail was a man with a rifle.

'Get down off the horse and throw

your guns to one side.'

The Kid considered the matter for an instant, then reached for his Winchester. There was a loud crack and he fell to the ground, blood streaming from his leg. He tried to move but there was no way he could stand. He managed to slither forward a few inches till he came in contact with a pair of boots. Looking up through pain-filled eyes he saw a man standing over him. He tried to figure who it was but he didn't recognize him.

'Who in hell are you?' he murmured.

'The name's Ahiga. You don't know me. You or your boys stole some of my sheep. I guess you won't be doin' it again.'

*   *   *

It had been another hot day in Hackberry and evening was drawing down as Marshal Shackleton locked the door of his office. He had just made a final check on the Ocotillo Kid, who

214

was laid up in the jail-house with his leg in a plaster. Together with a couple of his outlaw gang, he would remain there till the arrival of the circuit judge. Waiting for the marshal outside were Somersby and his niece, together with Fogarty and Ahiga. The deputy marshal's right arm was in a sling but his left encircled Cora's waist.

'OK,' Shackleton said, 'I don't know about you folk, but I figure I've had about enough for today.'

Cora giggled. 'Uncle,' she said, 'this must be the quietest day you've had for a long time.'

'I didn't appreciate how much paperwork it took till now,' Shackleton replied. He glanced at Somersby. 'I figure you arranged it for your right arm to be the one out of action.'

'I reckon I could manage with the left,' Somersby said.

The marshal grinned. 'Looks like you're doin' just that,' he said. 'No, I think we all deserve a rest. And we got things to celebrate.' They began to make their way down the quiet street in the direction of the marshal's house.

'Is Taggart OK?' Shackleton asked.

'Sure. He got badly concussed but he's fine. He's back at your place cookin' up somethin' for us right now.'

'Are you sure you don't mind havin' us around for a while?' Fogarty said.

'Quite sure. You're all very welcome to stay just as long as you like. I don't know what plans you have, but take your time thinkin' about 'em.'

'If what Arrowsmith said is true,' Fogarty said, 'it seems like there could be silver up in the Senita River country.'

'You figure on goin' prospectin' again?' Shackleton asked.

'Nope, not me. But if Taggart won't be goin' back to the Blister Beetle, he might be interested in takin' on that old mine. If it works out, it could ensure the future for Somersby and Cora, for all of you.'

'You talk as if it don't concern you and Ahiga.'

Fogarty laughed. 'Me and Ahiga ain't

no miners,' he said. 'Nope, if there's silver, you're welcome to it.'

'So what will you do?'

'I got a place of my own,' Ahiga said. 'Now that we've dealt with the Ocotillo Kid, I aim to go back.' He looked at his friend. 'I reckon you might make a decent sheepherder,' he said.

Again Fogarty laughed. 'Maybe,' he said. 'Who knows?'

'Why not stay in Hackberry?' Cora said. She was suddenly enthusiastic. 'Why don't we all stay in Hackberry? It would be so nice.'

'There goes the voice of youth,' Shackleton said. 'You hardly know the place yet, Cora. In fact, we've hardly got to know each other.'

'I've got to know all I really want to know,' Cora replied, looking from her uncle to Somersby. They continued walking and were soon approaching the marshal's house.

'Seems like a long time since I first rode into town,' Fogarty said. He and the marshal exchanged glances and grinned. 'A whole heap of things have happened since then. I think Shackleton's right. Let's just ease off and see how things go.'

They walked up the path. Shackleton opened the door and sniffed.

'I don't know what Taggart's been cookin' up,' he said, 'but it sure smells good. Come on in. Make yourselves at home, folks.'

THE END